**"I can take you..."** she managed to say.

Ty nuzzled the back of Kenzie's neck. "Not if I take you first."

His words fed a primal need in her to be claimed, while her mind screamed they were in public, could be seen. And wasn't that the crux of involvement with Ty? There was always a risk, always that telltale touch of spontaneity that was his calling card, that thing that always made sex as fun as it was pleasurable.

"When did little Kenzie Malone decide she liked the risk of getting caught?" he whispered, his lips barely brushing the top of her ear.

"If you'd park your boots beside the bed for longer than a couple of hours, I would imagine there would be a lot you'd learn about the women you take to bed, Covington, including me." He snapped his head back. "That's what I thought," she murmured, pulling on her arms.

And like every other experience she'd had with him, he let go and was out the door before she could ask him to stay.

Dear Reader,

As I wrote this story, I found myself often grieving the fact that this is the end of the Covington brothers' stories. There is something inherently poignant about writing the last book in a trilogy, particular when the story centers around characters as tightly knit as these men. They've been so much fun to write and even more fun to share with you as the stories built and the world grew.

I do have a confession, though. Despite the fact I'm the author and should, in theory, know how the story goes, Ty's story presented a handful of surprises as I wrote—some heartbreaking before they could be happy. This posed some challenges, and I had a blast making it all work. (And rest easy—Ty and Kenzie end up with exactly what they need.) The experience created a final product I was—and am—able to look at with pride. This is a series that will forever hold a special place in my heart. Seeing the brothers find success and love has been an absolute thrill.

I want to thank you for riding along.

And while this is the last book for the Covington brothers, wise words from a fellow author helped remind me that this isn't over. The brothers will live on every time someone picks up one of their stories. And there are always the ranch hands who have stories to tell...

Happy reading,

*Kelli Ireland*

# Kelli Ireland

———

## Cowboy Strong

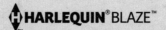

HARLEQUIN® BLAZE™

Recycling programs
for this product may
not exist in your area.

ISBN-13: 978-0-373-79890-2

Cowboy Strong

Copyright © 2016 by Denise Tompkins

Printed in U.S.A.

**Kelli Ireland** spent a decade as a name on a door in corporate America. Unexpectedly liberated by Fate's sense of humor, she chose to carpe the diem and pursue her passion for writing. A fan of happily-ever-afters, she found she loved being the puppet master for the most unlikely couples. Seeing them through the best and worst of each other while helping them survive the joys and disasters of falling in love? Best. Thing. Ever. Visit Kelli's website at kelliireland.com.

### Books by Kelli Ireland

### Harlequin Blaze

#### *Pleasure Before Business*

*Stripped Down*
*Wound Up*
*Pulled Under*

#### *Wild Western Heat*

*A Cowboy Returns*
*Cowboy Proud*

To get the inside scoop on Harlequin Blaze and its talented writers, be sure to check out BlazeAuthors.com.

All backlist available in ebook format.

Visit the Author Profile page at
Harlequin.com for more titles.

To my father-in-law,

a large-animal veterinarian who looks and sounds enough like Sam Elliott to terrify folks. I think it's the mustache.

I've got your number, though. Ranger cookies.

Love you.

# *1*

TYSON COVINGTON LEANED against the end of the trailer and waited on the person he considered his personal dealer in ecstasy to deliver. It wasn't as though he was addicted. He could stop any time he wanted to. He just didn't want to. The level of feel-good that was about to change hands was insane. And *cheap*. It could be worse. *Much* worse.

"Number seventy-two," the matronly woman in the portable kitchen called as she slid his order through the trailer's narrow delivery window and across the short counter. "Funnel cake, extra powdered sugar, and a large lemonade."

Ty stepped around the corner of the trailer. "Thank you, ma'am." He tipped his hat to her before tucking the plastic cup between his arm and body, juggling the grease-stained paper plate in his hands.

If he ever met a woman who could whip these up for him? His single days would be over. For regular funnel cake access, even *he* would consider marriage.

A large barn fan kicked on and swept away the extra

powered sugar. Ty clutched his plate tighter as the dense cloud of sugary goodness dissipated in the air.

Ty tore off a wedge of the hot treat and shoved it in his mouth. Sucking in a breath at the burn, he inhaled a lungful of powdered sugar. All the willpower in the world couldn't stop him from choking. He coughed hard and blew out what looked like a face full of illegal substance all over the back of a nearby cowboy's dark denim shirt.

*Oops.*

Still, he wasn't about to let something as ridiculous as a second-degree burn to the mouth or a personal confrontation destroy the pleasure of the first bite. There was something about rodeos that just made funnel cakes taste better.

He glanced around and let the sights, sounds and smells momentarily take him over. Man, he loved rodeos. Listening to the scratchy amplification of the announcer's voice boom over the subtle, hive-like hum of the crowded stable area, Ty thought that was probably how God sounded as He called out the scores for those entering heaven horseback. And if, for some reason, Ty couldn't enter heaven horseback? He wasn't sure he wanted to go.

Shod hooves hit the dirt pack with sharp clips as owners unloaded horses nearby. Others were arranging stalls, wiping down hides until they shone under the lights and generally working with their animals. Some—both animals and owners alike—were high-strung. Others were old pros, comfortable with the routine common to every competition. Even one with stakes as high as this. The banter between the cowboys, half bragging and half bullshit, resulted in sharp laughs now and again.

Ty relaxed a bit.

He wandered into the community barn and stopped in front of the stall he'd been assigned. Shifting to lean against the bottom half of the Dutch door, he chewed rapidly and tried to breathe with more care—in through the nose, out through the mouth. His eyes still watered enough his vision blurred. Yeah, he could've taken a big swallow of lemonade, but he wasn't a wuss. Besides, some things were simply sacrosanct. Funnel cakes were up there on that list, so he'd eat his cake like a grown man or not at all.

Gingerly shifting the paper plate around, he took a second bite. The first burn was bad enough that the second and then third hardly registered. Glancing around, he took a healthy swallow of lemonade, his shoulders sagging as the cold assuaged the scalding heat.

*Still not a wuss, since no one witnessed the momentary weakness.*

A dark velvet nose slipped over his shoulder and huffed, sending the plate—and the treat—flipping end over end out of his hand. The plate rolled away and came to a stop next to a bale of hay. The delicacy hit the hard-packed dirt with a *thwap*—facedown.

Tyson glanced over his shoulder at the big, wide eyes—one brown, one blue—doing their best to appear innocent and full of curiosity. He scowled. "Don't look at me as if you were being deprived, you big mule. You *know* I would've shared a bite when it cooled off."

The horse flapped his lips at his owner in a not-so-subtle demand.

Fighting a grin, Ty picked up the cake and retrieved the plate, gently slapping the two together to knock away most of the dirt before tearing off dusty chunks and feeding them to his horse, Doc Bar's Dippy Zippy Gizmo. But as far as the ladies were concerned, he went by Gizmo. The stud horse had the disposition of a labradoodle crossed with a bullmastiff—gentle, playful, loving and strong as an ox with a heart that just wouldn't quit. He was also developing quite the reputation with breeders in the area for passing on both his disposition and superior skills to his get. Demand had become so intense eighteen months ago that Ty had put the horse on a breeding hiatus. He hadn't wanted to, but he couldn't keep up the breeding demand and the competitive circuit. One or the other had to give.

The stud horse was only six years old. On the fringes of entering his prime, as far as competition went, and the idea of pulling him off the rodeo circuit when he'd really begun to shine seemed incredibly unfair to both of them. They'd worked hard to earn the points, and money, necessary to make it onto the pro roster. That had been followed by hard work and a lot of long hours in the truck and trailer as they traversed the country, attending every event they could. The end goal had always been the same—earning a spot on the National Cutting Horse Association national finals roster and a chance at the more than four million dollars in prize money.

It still didn't feel real.

Winning would entitle Ty to demand premiums for Gizmo's stud services, to be even more selective in breeding and creating the Covington line of Quarter horses, a line he'd named Bar None. Like Doc Bar before him, Gizmo was the seat of what Ty was determined would go down in the Quarter Horse Hall of Fame as one of the finest lines ever.

He didn't want to create a mass-market Quarter horse.

He wanted exclusivity, a name for his horse and himself, a legacy that would make him his own man, no longer overshadowed by his brothers.

Ty was pulled from his thoughts as a crowd of spectators walked by the stables discussing the horses and their odds. It didn't matter that it was December in Fort Worth, Texas. People from around the world had flown in for this. They'd hang out, see the city's sights and spend a little money. But come tomorrow, these same people would be in the stands, cheering on the stars of the rodeo circuit.

On the streets, limousines ferried international horse breeders and buyers—men and women who Ty hoped would come out to watch Gizmo in action and see what Ty had worked so hard to cultivate in the genetics program he'd started in his teens. They would watch with the open intent of either investing capital in Ty's program or passing on him.

*No. Pressure.*

Ty shook his head. Thinking that way gained him nothing. What he *needed* to do was focus on Gizmo, keep him healthy and happy and energized. The horse was nearly psychic. If he sensed Ty was off, the two would end up out of sync, and that wouldn't serve either of them well. That meant Ty had to find that inner place where he could simply exist, the place he'd spent so much time as a child, the place no one could reach him.

But his mind threw one more curveball before he could shut himself down. What if he actually took the top title? The little bit of funnel cake he'd eaten wadded up into a thick lump and sank deep in his gut, settling like a ship's anchor. If he won, the recognition would take him places he'd dreamed of going all his life.

Ty studied his horse with a critical eye. Known as a grullo, Gizmo was a rare dun color—deep blue-gray body; black mane, tail and leg markings; a black dorsal stripe; and a pale face mask. Gizmo often sired colts with dun coloring thanks to a rare genetic marker, and as his predictability in colt color went up, so did the stud fees Ty could charge. Grullos were rare. Every dime of that money helped fund Ty's breeding program as well as his ability to travel the rodeo circuit and pay the exorbitant entry fees, not to mention helping cover the costs of hiring extra cowboys to cover him at his family's dude ranch. But what mattered most was Gizmo. Ty had loved the lunk since the colt had taken to following him around only a few days after birth.

"Doesn't seem to matter where we are. I always find you making moon eyes at that damn horse," said a highly familiar, decidedly feminine voice, coming from a dozen or so feet to his left.

Ty's lips twitched as his body came to life, fueled by raw awareness. "Not true."

"How do you figure?"

He ran his fingers into Gizmo's forelock and scratched. The horse's eyes drifted half closed. Ty glanced toward his stable neighbor, lifting a single brow as he offered a lazy smile. "Sometimes he makes moon eyes at *me*."

Mackenzie Malone, heiress to the Malone Quarter horse breeding empire and the most challenging competitor in the arena, considered him openly. Then she slipped into her horse's stall, disappearing from view. "Disturbingly true," she called, her voice muffled by the thick wooden wall that separated them. "True enough, in fact, that I'm not exactly sure how to reply."

"I would say that depends on whether or not you're

still seeing that suit. What was his name? It was a city...
Kincaid? Watson? Portland? Nashville?"

"His name was Dallas." Thick walls or not, her
amused response came through loud and clear.

"Still seeing him?" he pressed. It took a few minutes
for her to stick her head around the corner and answer
with a grin. Every second he waited deepened his vague
but persistent unease.

"Nope. Turns out he had a very weird penchant for...
Never mind. The answer is no. I'm not dating the city
boy anymore." One eye narrowed. "Why?"

Desire for the fiery redhead quickened his pulse,
prompting Ty to move away from Gizmo and peer into
Mackenzie's—Kenzie's—stall as she moved back inside. "Just want to make sure you know there's no need
to be jealous of Gizmo, darlin'. Since you're city-free,
I'll let you make moon eyes at me anytime."

"'Let me,' huh?" Her laugh was rich yet delicate, the
sound enticingly deceptive. She might look like a fragile waif and sound like an angel, but she was a powerful threat in the arena and hell's own temptress between
the sheets. "Keep dreaming, Covington. I don't make
moon eyes for anyone, but particularly for bed partners
who park their boots by the door instead of under the
bed with the intent to stay awhile."

He hadn't heard her complain before. Their long-
standing history in the arena had always been fun.
Before a rodeo, they'd establish the ground rules, the
winner gaining something he, or she, wanted to experience together, though it had always been in bed. These
postcompetition hookups allowed him to blow off a little
steam and manage any residual adrenaline and ramped-
up aggression after the long days on the rodeo circuit.

He and Kenzie had skipped a few opportunities to knock boots in the past, but only when one or the other was temporarily involved with someone else. And it was *always* temporary. Neither of them was programmed for long-term relationships, and that was what he adored about her. No expectations, no threat to either's independence and no hard feelings when he and Gizmo took home the top prize instead of her and her mare, Search for Independence, or Indie, which they did more often than not.

Still…here they were, chasing each other for spots in the finals, knowing they'd likely end up in a face-off at some point in the competition.

Ty absently pulled a piece of a gum out of his shirt pocket, his mind shifting to the first elimination early tomorrow morning.

Gizmo tossed his head and bugled, knocking one front hoof against the stall door, his eyes never leaving the sweet treat Ty held between two fingers.

"Fine. Take it. Your breath is horrible anyway." He handed the horse a piece of bubble gum and fought not to laugh as Gizmo seemed to grin, delicately plucking the treat from Ty's fingertips.

"Sometimes I wonder if Gizmo realizes you're more than a walking, talking soda jerk of sugary goodness."

Gizmo shoved him hard with his nose. Ty stepped away, just out of reach of the horse's flapping lips. "Enough," he mumbled, gently pushing Gizmo's face from his shirt pocket. "You're embarrassing me."

The horse tossed his head and continued to chew his gum with exaggerated enthusiasm.

Unfurling the in-stall water hose, Kenzie filled Indie's water buckets, watching to ensure the mare didn't step on the hose as she moved around, inspecting the new space.

"So," Kenzie called out to Ty, "how's the dude ranch endeavor going?"

Ty leaned against Indie's stall door. "It's been far more successful than we thought it would be, actually." They'd have to have another two years before they were in the black regularly. No way was he revealing that to a Malone, though. Wouldn't surprise him if her family lit winter fires with random dollar bills they had lying around their ranch. Kenzie had never known the hand-to-mouth existence he'd lived for a large part of his life. She couldn't understand.

Shaking off the discomfort of the chasm of differences in their socioeconomic positions, Ty continued, "Cade's fiancée has been amazing at getting us prime advertising and exposure. Thanks to her efforts, we were rated a five-star resort. She's pretty great."

"I heard Cade had popped the question." She twisted the spigot off before coiling the hose. "You like her?"

"I do. Quite a bit, actually. She's just what he needed." From any other woman, Ty would have weighed the comment for its jealousy component. Not with Kenzie. She was far too practical, and for that he was grateful. But it wasn't gratitude that resulted in the small twinge of emotion that pricked his heart. Truth? He had no idea what it was. And he had no intention of putting it under his internal microscope for evaluations. Some things were better off left alone, and this was one of those things. Besides, there was a bigger elephant standing between them.

He intended to take the title at this rodeo, and probably from this very woman.

KENZIE MALONE MOVED through Indie's stall with the ease born of thousands of hours doing the same repetitive tasks for a variety of horses, some of them hers but most her father's. Indie was all hers, though, and the mare was special. She was one of the first fillies out of a line Kenzie had started the moment she'd received the first half of her trust six years ago. She'd been eighteen.

The animal was an anomaly at five years old. Indie possessed more intuition, more instinctive responses than could be cataloged. Riding her was a dream. All Kenzie had to do was keep one leg on each side of the saddle and park her mind in the middle. The horse did the rest. Indie knew where to step, when and why, and that left Kenzie with less to do than fans might believe. Yet riding Indie always provided a thrill—almost as much as the man currently lingering in the doorway.

Every inch of Ty Covington's six-three frame was delectable. She wanted to run her tongue through the hollow at the base of his throat…again. She wanted to taste the salt and sunshine on his skin…again. She wanted to nibble her way to the waistline of his jeans and dip her fingers below the band of his boxer briefs, tease the root of his arousal before taking him…again.

It dawned on Kenzie that she should probably spare them both the public humiliation and turn the hose on herself before she mentally stripped Ty naked. Face flushed, she pulled her hat off and ran Indie's polishing rag over her head, wiping away the excess sweat. Not much she could do about the shortness of breath or the way her nipples pearled beneath her T-shirt. That was simply the way she responded to Ty. Each time. Every time.

Aware it wouldn't take the man long to pick up on her

interest, she focused on tasks that would keep the horse between them. But Ty, being Ty, managed to charm the female in Indie, moving her away from her hay net to accept the small pieces of apple Ty offered. The horse's move left Kenzie with a head-to-toe view of the cowboy.

She was torn between thanking the gods for his perfection and cursing the same deities for the distraction the man created by simply *being*. Broad shoulders, a muscular build, dirty-blond hair that was a good four weeks past the point of trimming, brown eyes richer than the most expensive chocolate, large hands, strong jaw and lips made for kissing—all things that drew her. But what really flipped her switch was his confidence. True confidence, though, not arrogance.

For a man who looked the way he did and had so many notches in his bedpost it resembled a totem pole, that was saying something. And as if that weren't attractive enough, she had to include his sense of humor, compassion, friendliness and easy compatibility—in public, but particularly in private. It was the recipe for the perfect man. Or would have been, save one thing.

Tyson Covington couldn't stand postsex *anything*. No cuddling. No pillow talk. She'd never had the chance to wake up to his sleep-rumpled face the next morning because he'd *never* spent the night. He made a mad dash for the door before she could ask him to stay. It had started out as a relief. Now? Kenzie wasn't as comfortable about his urgency to get out of her room once they were both satisfied. And it was *always* her room.

She turned away from him, worrying her bottom lip with such ferocity it hurt.

"It's not like you to turn your back on me, Malone." From her peripheral vision, she watched the man step closer and tip the brim of his hat up to better reveal those dark brown eyes. "What's bothering you?"

The simple question, so softly worded, totally caught her off guard. He'd always been playful. This quiet concern was new, and it threw her off her game. It was the only reason she had for answering, "Just thinking."

"About?"

"You." Heat rushed across her cheeks. This wasn't how they worked, and she doubted he'd take the change well.

She didn't see him move, but suddenly he'd spun her around and pressed the front of her body against the darkest corner of the stall wall. Running his hands up her arms, he stretched her out, her wrists captured in one hand.

Kenzie yanked on her wrists and arched her back.

Ty kicked her feet wide and, bending at the knees, rubbed the ridge of his impressive erection up and down the seam of her ass. Bending forward to cover her, his lips brushed the edge of her ear as he spoke. "Ground rules stay the same as those we set at regionals. Winner gets his—or her—fantasy night. Or do you want to modify the game for the big show?"

His hot breath tickled her ear and made her shiver.

Her body responded of its own accord, her back arching again to better present her ass, her arms pulling against his hands, her head canting farther to the side so he might have better access to her neck. His actions fed a primal need in her to be taken, claimed, while her mind screamed that they were in public, could be caught. And wasn't that the crux of being with Ty? There was always a risk, always that touch of spontaneity that was his calling card, that thing that always made sex as fun as it was pleasurable.

Ty let her neck go without warning. Then he stretched her arms higher, forcing her to move to follow them up the wall. "When did little Kenzie Malone decide she liked a little exhibitionism?" he whispered, moist lips barely brushing the top of her ear.

"When did the cowboy who established *love 'em and leave 'em* decide to stick around long enough to do it right?" she countered.

Ty grabbed her hip and spun her to face him. Wedging a thigh between her legs, he rubbed against her sex with firm strokes. Not once did he tear his gaze from hers. "Where's this coming from, Kenzie?"

"If you'd park your boots beside the bed instead of being so damn afraid to take them off at all, I would imagine there would be a lot you'd learn about the women you call 'lover,' Covington. Including me." The brazen statement held within it a poorly disguised challenge, one he clearly heard.

He hauled his body back, eyes wide, and let go of her arms before spinning for the door and stalking out.

She never had the chance to ask him to stay.

# 2

THE NIGHT WAS passing slower than any Ty could remember. The second hand on the clock ticked and paused, ticked and paused, seemingly searching for the energy to tick again. He tossed and turned, went down to check on Gizmo, then went back up to his hotel room to toss and turn again. He needed to blow off a little steam, and sex was his preferred method.

And his mind was locked on one particular redhead, a woman he'd had numerous times but never could get out of his system.

It wasn't as though Ty was actually into exhibitionism. He'd just wanted to push the fringes of experience and try something new, and she'd always been safe—as well as seriously fun—to play with. And bless the powers that be, darling Kenzie hadn't balked. His pulse quickened. Hell, if anything, she'd asked him for more. But he hadn't been certain how much "more" was wise in the barn.

He'd also had a fleeting moment of insecurity, wondering if she'd want more of what he'd offered just then or more of him in general. The former he could provide, and gladly. He'd always liked women, had always been insistent that everyone left satisfied. But him offering more than what the moment afforded all parties? No. That type of "more" had never been on the table. Ever.

His rolled over and punched his pillow.

Earlier, the competitors had drawn for their bracket positions, and he'd drawn third out of fifty riders. It was a crappy pick. He'd have much preferred to ride somewhere between thirtieth and thirty-fifth so he knew how hard to push Gizmo and how much showmanship was required to keep his horse in the top ten while still preserving enough energy to really clean up if he was called to a tiebreaker.

Flopping onto his back, he stared at the shadowed ceiling. Insomnia sucked. Bad. Insomnia alone sucked worse. He really needed some feminine company to get his mind off all the people who'd be watching him and Gizmo, both live and on TV. The pressure of those anticipated stares grew heavy in the silence, then heavier still, until he thought he might not be able to draw a breath due to the weight on his chest.

The bedcovers tangled around his feet as he lurched upward. He got his feet underneath him, shoved his room key in the pocket of the complimentary robe before tugging it on and then grabbed his cell as he headed for the door.

He hit 6 on speed dial and waited as the call connected. When she answered, he let out a breath he hadn't realized he'd been holding.

"Why are you calling me—" covers rustled and her jaw cracked as she yawned "—at one thirty in the morning?"

Thoughts of her in bed, her lithe body clad in little—or nothing—made him adjust his robe for better coverage. "What room are you in?"

"You're looking for a booty call from the wrong woman. I'm sleeping."

"You lost the wager." He spoke so fast his words ran together.

Silence.

"I beat you at regionals, so I entered nationals with a points lead. Means I get my fantasy fulfilled first," he pressed.

"We aren't on the boards yet."

Her cautious tone worried him, made his response sharper than he'd intended. "Actually, we are. I went to check on Gizmo and Indie earlier tonight, make sure they were settled, and end-of-season scores have been posted."

"Well," she mused, "I suppose that puts you on top of me."

His cock kicked hard enough there was no hiding it. Thankfully, the hallway was empty. "On top's not where I want to be."

She chuckled, the sound sleep heavy, sultry. "You realize that if I beat you here, I'll top you in points and earnings for the year."

His brow creased. "No. Just until the next rodeo season starts."

"Not by your logic. You're saying you get to have your fantasy tonight because you're ahead in points in a competition that hasn't started. Well, this exact same competition won't start again until December next year, so I could feasibly be ahead of you in points until they post next year's regional totals on the nationals boards. Same thing you're doing, just building out the timeline."

His mouth went dry and he stopped, resting his shoulder against the wall. "You're making me think this was a bad idea."

"Good or bad, it was *your* idea, Tyson," she said softly. "Room 1134. Show up and own it, or hang up and don't. But make up your mind in the next five minutes or I'm going back to sleep and I won't answer after that. Not the phone, and definitely not the door."

The line went dead. If he showed up now, he'd be accepting the fact that she was right—his terms had been pretty broad and rather unclear. If she beat him, could she, *would* she, want to see him for the next year? That would take this thing between them outside their established bounds of competition romps. Make it more than an occasional tryst. As in…dating.

The idea didn't repel him, and that alone should have been enough to turn him right around and have him back in his room before he lost what was left of his mind.

He decided not to give the thought too much attention, though, so he pushed off the wall and resumed his trek toward the elevator bank.

He reached the elevators just as one opened and dumped off a group of highly intoxicated bridesmaids supporting one barely conscious bride. To a woman, they looked him over as if he were the best thing they'd seen all night. While he wasn't entirely comfortable with it, he still smiled and flirted a little before stepping into the elevator car and winking at them as the doors closed. It was, after all, what anyone who knew him would have expected of him.

He punched the button for the eleventh floor and ignored the way his belly dipped as the car started its upward climb.

Because he knew with the kind of certainty that discomfited a man that the belly drop had nothing to do with the elevator and everything to do with the woman in room 1134.

KENZIE HAD BEEN fast asleep when her cell phone rang. Part of her had known before squinting at the bright caller ID who it would be. The other part of her had grumbled and threatened to go back to sleep, right up to the point she swiped the answer button on the screen and heard Ty's voice. His seductive teasing? Pretty much expected. Lust swamping her like a johnboat with a cannonball hole in its center? Not so much.

After disconnecting the call, she lay there considering her parting shot. *He's not going to show up after I challenged him like that.*

She had no idea where the idea to challenge him had come from. She'd only known she wasn't about to simply roll over and let him have his way with her because he was coiled tighter than a self-winding watch on an MMA fighter's wrist. It didn't matter that she wanted him just as bad and was wound just as tight. The principle of the thing mattered—the principle and their agreement.

Well, that added to the fact that he wasn't one to fish the same pond over and over if the catch was too easy. He needed the challenge, and it had to come across as near defiance if a woman thought to reel him in for even a single passionate night.

And she posed a more authentic challenge than most.

What she needed was to have a quality man chasing her, not someone simply after the Malone name or associated fortune. As the sole Malone heir, she'd learned this lesson by age fourteen.

At fifteen, Jack Malone, her father and her idol, had pulled her aside to administer some of the best advice Kenzie had ever received. "When we lost your brother, others assumed I'd want another son to pass the Malone legacy on to, but you know—" he'd gripped her arms "—you *know* I wouldn't trade you for all the Spanish gold hidden in the ocean's depths. And when it comes to taking a man as husband, I won't make that choice for you. I don't care if the man you fall in love with is an artist, a pilot, a musician, a doctor or a garbageman. I set your trust up for you to be well-off, so your man doesn't have to be rolling in money to make you happy." He'd taken her by the shoulders then, his grip just this side of painful. "I have loved your mother through both lean years and flush times. Money can't make a marriage, let alone a *happy* marriage," he'd said softly before clearing his throat, voice gruff when he'd refocused on Kenzie. "You find the man you want to wake up to for the rest of your life, the man you can't help but give your heart to, and you marry *him*. Just promise me you won't elope, baby girl. You're my one shot to publicly blubber as father of the bride."

Now here she was, waiting on a man she desired and equally admired to come to her room at her invitation. "Sheer irony. Nothing more," she whispered, stretching her clasped hands above her head. She should probably brush her hair before—

The rap at her door, soft but firm, had her throwing the covers back at the same time her heart lodged itself in her throat. *He showed up.* She wouldn't overanalyze it, wouldn't overthink it. She'd just enjoy it.

Padding across the room in her cami and thong, she peered through the peephole and bit her bottom lip. Ty stood there, hands in his pockets, and grinned at her. That man wore a borrowed robe better than anyone she'd ever seen. "Hopeless," she muttered, unsure whether it was him she spoke about or herself.

She opened the door.

Ty slipped inside, bare feet silent on the carpet. He swiftly shut the door and, grabbing her around the waist, spun and pressed her against the wall. Lips, full but soft, teased along her jaw, and he whispered, "Missed you."

*Don't believe him*, her mind volunteered. *You're no one special to him. After all, he's known as the Rodeo Romeo.*

She stiffened.

Lifting his head to stare down at her, Ty's gaze roamed her face. "Something wrong?"

"No." She smiled absently. "I'm good."

He curled a finger under her chin and lifted until met his stare. "Surely you can do better than that."

"It's the middle of the night, Ty. 'Good' is pretty damn spectacular."

He laughed quietly, pulling her into his arms and backing her to the bed. "I'll do my best to make sure you don't regret answering your phone."

"Your first task is keeping me awake."

He nipped her ear. "This is my fantasy, Malone. That starts with you being awake and receptive to my cunning seduction."

"And it ends with?"

Again he lifted his head, but all signs of teasing

had disappeared. Dark brown eyes bored into hers, the weight of their intent scattering goose bumps along her skin. "It ends with you screaming my name."

Her mouth formed a small O, but no sound emerged. She was too surprised at his directness to utter anything more than the most fundamental thought. "When did you get so serious about sex?"

Ty leaned forward, his lips brushing hers as soft as a butterfly's caress. "When you answered your phone. I need you as much as I want you tonight, Mackenzie."

The way her name rolled so richly off his tongue made her whimper.

She should answer. She really should. But the words were stuck in her throat behind her thundering heart.

*He wants me,* needs *me.*

Never had he admitted to anything more than "craving" her. The hunger to hear him confess it again almost had her asking for him to repeat his words, but pride intervened. Then he slid a hand between them, deft fingers manipulating her sex with skill born of experience, and all thoughts of admissions evaporated. Heat built between them faster than sheer winds from a prairie storm's dry line. He'd never been this way with her, never been anything more than a fun bed partner she enjoyed when their paths crossed and she was in the mood. This man? He was different, in control, almost predatory. Closing her eyes, she gripped the looped cotton weave of his robe and let her head fall back, gasping slightly when he laid his lips to the hollow of her throat.

His huffed out a small laugh against her skin. The smell of mint hit her—*toothpaste*—as his breath wafted up, strong and clean.

"Kiss me," she murmured, tossing his hat aside in order to run her fingers through his hair.

"Demanding little thing," he answered, weaving a hand of his own through her mass of curls and fisting it in her hair just tight enough her eyes widened. He stared at her for several seconds before placing his cheek next to hers, so close that his lips caressed her ear as he spoke. "Tonight's my fantasy. You agreed to the terms when I called. Clear?"

"You going to bite me again?" she asked, exhaling slowly.

"Absolutely."

"Then, hell yes, we're clear, but only if you quit stalling."

Ty chuckled as he shrugged out of his robe and stood before her, gloriously nude and unashamed of his body. His abs tightened as she touched the muscled ridges and valleys, tracing the chiseled six-pack of his torso, the ropy lengths of muscle in his arms and the corded strength in his legs. The way his lats cut down his abs and framed his long, thick arousal. She let her gaze linger there, and that seemed to be his undoing.

Scooping her up, he sank onto the bed and rolled to his back, placing her on top of him. He ran a hand around the back of her neck and pulled her down as he rose toward her. Stopping millimeters from their mouths colliding, his hot breath washed over her.

She licked her bottom lip. They were so close her tongue brushed over the soft skin of his full lower lip. The faint taste of mint lingered there as the scent did on his breath.

Ty's eyes flared, pupils dilated as he closed the last of the distance between them, claiming her mouth without hesitation. Tongues dueled, lips sucked and harsh breaths wound together in something akin to demands, not requests, made by desperate lovers.

It was a war she wanted to fight forever, one she might never want to win.

Lying back, he encouraged her to straddle his hips. He bent his knees, pushing her forward. Her dark red curls fell in a curtain around them to create the sensation they were cocooned, the world forever far away. He broke this kiss, the rapid rise and fall of his chest mirroring hers. "Hell's fires, woman. Give a man a chance."

Kenzie traced his bottom lip with her thumb, clenching her thighs around his hips when he nipped her finger. "Chance to what?"

"Seduce you." In a swift move, he rolled her over. "It was supposed to be a drawn-out seduction, with me doing the seducing."

"And…" Kenzie prompted.

"I'm the one being seduced. Your mouth should come with a warning label."

"It does," she said, lowering her face to his and kissing him slowly this time, in a leisurely exploration, tasting him, sipping from his mouth, running her hands over his pecs and wrapping her legs around his waist.

He broke away only to bury his face in the crook of her neck. "You wreck me."

"And that's a bad thing?" she teased, tracing her fingers lightly down his rib cage.

Ty sucked in a breath and shivered. Without looking, he reached over the edge of the bed and dug through his robe, retrieving a condom. "I can't wait, Kenzie. I wanted to, but this first time is going to be rough, fast. I need…" He shrugged, fumbling with the wrapper until, cursing, he sat back on his knees and sheathed his length. "I really want…" he began again.

Those words again—*need, want*—used in relation to her. "We're dancing to the same tune, Ty."

Eyes narrowing and mouth tightening to a thin line, he took her arm and gently pulled. "Roll over." She followed his direction only to have him grasp her hips and lift. "On your knees, Mackenzie."

She'd barely assumed the position when he pulled her down his entire length with enough strength to make her cry out with a surprised thrill. "Tyson!"

He pushed her shoulders to the mattress. "Arms wide."

She complied, but slowly, earning a quick slap to the ass that set more than her skin on fire. He rubbed his hand over the stinging skin and whispered words of encouragement to her. Then he began to thrust and retreat. All she could do was feel, experience and indulge in Tyson.

His fingers dug into her hips as he pumped faster. "Hold on to the sheets and don't let go."

Arching her back and lifting her rear higher earned his praise as well as a heartfelt curse. "Can't…baby… I can't…" He reached around her and found her clitoris, manipulating it almost frantically as the arm that held him up shook and his rhythm faltered.

Orgasm crashed into her and she offered his name to the heavens in a soulful cry, his voice joining hers. Their fingers wove together, tightening, as they grounded each other through the emotional onslaught.

When it passed, Kenzie relaxed her hand and made to turn over, but Ty gently lowered himself onto her back. "You know better than to think we're done, darlin'."

"It's late, Ty," she contentedly murmured into the pillow.

He rained kisses all over her shoulders. "It's never too late for round two, Mackenzie."

Hiding her face in her pillow, she smiled.

That was exactly what she'd hoped he'd say.

# 3

TY LET KENZIE drift off to sleep around 4:30 a.m. before quietly gathering his things to leave. Door open, the light from the hallway cutting through the room's darkness, he glanced back. She looked like a fallen angel with her nude body spread across the bed, lips kiss swollen and hair in disarray. Long lashes fluttered against her cheeks and opened enough to reveal the brilliant blue of her eyes. Her soft sigh revealed her immediate understanding that he was leaving.

Normally that would be Ty's cue to go. But there was something about Kenzie, something about the way she'd given herself to him tonight, that rode his conscience. For the first time, Ty wanted to stay, to see the night through and wake up to her face in the morning. It was the strangest sensation, this foreign need to wake up with a woman in his arms. Not just any woman, but *this* woman.

He strode back to the bed. Ignoring her unguarded surprise, he bent over her and kissed her, all tongue and teeth and heat. She responded, arching into the hand he placed on her breast and wrapping a hand around the arm parked next to her head.

The ever-simmering ember of desire that lay between them fanned to life, the flame licking at the base of his spine as his shaft thickened.

"Stay," she whispered against his mouth, tracing his bottom lip with the tip of her tongue.

He tried to imagine waking up to her beautiful face, tried to imagine her hair spread over his pillow. Sure, he could see it, but he could also imagine it being the beginning of something much larger, something he hadn't ever believed he would want. The longer he thought of the possible consequences, the more actively hesitation shoved at his willingness to try. It took only seconds for hesitation to win the battle, if not the war.

Ty stood. "I can't, darlin'. You know I've got to be up early." Without a word, she watched as he retied his robe with fumbling fingers. "I'll see you in the morning?"

Still, she said nothing.

He left as quickly as he'd arrived, anxiety driving him into the hall and all the way to his room. Whatever she'd wanted from him sexually, she'd definitely gotten. Beyond that? He refused to examine their exchange too closely.

Sleep dogged his heels when, several minutes later, he slipped into his room and quietly shut the door. He'd preset the alarm on his smartphone before knocking on Kenzie's door, ensuring he'd be up early enough he wouldn't have to rush to the barn. Shuffling through the dark room, he paused to set the desktop radio alarm as a backup, shed his robe and then collapsed onto his bed. The air conditioner's sharp *click* preceded the smell of refrigerated air, slightly canned and stale, as it swept across the room. For all that he preferred the outdoors, the artificially cooled air was bliss on his overheated skin. Air-conditioning always helped him sleep.

The robe tangled around his legs and he kicked at it even as he tried to retrieve the covers. No luck. The cooler he grew, the more determined he was to simply stop fighting and give in to sleep. Without at least a few z's, it would be pointless for him to show up in the arena in—he cracked one eye and peered at the clock—less than four hours. Gizmo deserved more than that from him. His eyes drifted shut.

Sometime later, he woke with a start and the absolute, sickening certainty he was late. A quick check of his watch proved his instincts right. Very. He glanced at the desktop clock and realized it was an hour slow. If he'd depended on that alarm alone, he'd have missed the competition altogether.

*My phone. Where the hell's my phone and why didn't that alarm go off?*

He'd last had his phone in his robe. He dug through the pockets. *Not there.*

Didn't matter. There wasn't time to hunt it down. The rules required him to be ready and warming up thirty minutes prior to his call time. He had less than an hour before he and Gizmo were due in the competition arena, less than twenty-five minutes before he had to be in the warm-up ring.

Yanking on jeans with one hand while he tried to pull on his shirt with the other proved fruitless and forced him to slow down. Man, he had *not* wanted to start nationals this way. He got himself together and sprinted from the room, rode the elevator to the lobby and raced through the crowds. He uttered apologies as he clipped folks left and right.

Another glance at his watch as he waited to cross the street to the temporary stalls said he had thirteen minutes to prep Gizmo and get him to the ring.

*Damn it. Not enough time.*

The light changed and he kicked into an all-out sprint through even heavier crowds. His stomach plummeted when—from twenty yards away—he saw the top of the Dutch door was already open. He slid to a stop in front of the stall...and gaped.

Kenzie stood there casually brushing the horse's tail. Gizmo had been saddled up, his reins looped over the wall-mounted hitching ring. His splint boots rested in the tack bucket she'd hauled out with her.

"What are you doing?" The question whipped across the distance, sharp enough to cause Gizmo to bob his head and paw the ground in protest.

"Why, I'm putting pretty polka-dot bows in your manly horse's tail before I paint his hooves 'I'm Not Really a Waitress' red by OPI, of course," Kenzie answered, just as brittle. "That way you might fool the steers, mesmerizing them with his handsome appearance. Just a hint? Right here, a 'thank you, Kenzie' wouldn't be inappropriate."

Ty stared at her, his eyebrows climbing into his hairline. "You're such a smart-ass." Grabbing the splints, he knelt in front of his horse and, moving quickly, yanked the Velcro straps in place.

"And you're behaving like a real jackass." She tossed the steel comb at him. "I came down to feed Indie and saw you hadn't taken care of Gizmo. The longer you went without showing up, the more I began to think it might be helpful if I lent a hand. I actually just called your cell to make sure you were up. My bad, seeing as you clearly have this under complete control. I suppose I should tell you to ignore the voice mail where I yell at you to get your butt in gear."

She moved past him and he instinctively stood and grabbed her arm. "I'm sorry."

"Yeah, you are," she bit out. "Now let go."

He tightened his hold. "No. Look, Kenzie. I'm truly sorry. You have to understand, I *need* this…"

Her brow furrowed when he trailed off. "Need what?"

He stopped himself just short of explaining the prize money was necessary for him to expand his breeding operation, and he was glad. As a Malone, she wouldn't understand his desperation to claim the prize money. It fueled his drive every day. Instead of answering, he shifted his approach. "I appreciate that you stepped in and helped." He shrugged, the skin across his shoulders tightening until it was too small to comfortably cover his large frame. "Thank you."

She eyed him with open disbelief, as if she knew it hadn't been what he'd started to say. In the end, though, she let it go with a "Sure. Whatever."

Ty moved around her to tighten Gizmo's cinch before he led the stud into the barn alley. "I hate to run, but I have to check in at the warm-up ring."

"Go. I'll be in the stands."

"Taking notes on how it's done?" he teased, mounting his horse.

"Nope. Watching arena conditions, checking out how worked up the steers get and gauging what the judges seem to be scoring on most heavily." She tapped her chin and then met his eyes, grinning. "Oh, yeah. And just how hard I have to bother to beat you."

Ty laughed. "One of the things I admire most about you, Malone, is your warped sense of entitlement." The minute the words left his mouth, he knew he'd stepped in it. Her face went stony and her spine ramrod straight. He opened his mouth to say something lighthearted, but she cut him off.

"I had no idea you thought so little of my skill, Covington." She crossed her arms under her chest and took a step away from Gizmo. "Normally I wouldn't address such nonsense, but this is one thing I'm compelled to settle. You may consider me 'entitled,' but I work every bit as hard as you do, if not harder. I put in just as many hours in the saddle, in the barn and on the computer to perfect my breeding program. No one can claim that's done with any sense of entitlement since I do it all myself. I'll pit my work ethic against yours *any* day."

She spun on her heel and stalked off, weaving through the crowd with a kind of fluid grace no one else had ever mimicked, let alone matched. For such a petite woman, she seemed taller, more sure of herself than ever. That she hadn't apologized for her legacy but rather had bitch-slapped him with it raised his opinion of her mightily. And that she'd walked away without sparing him a glance? He shouldn't find it sexy, but he did. Not many women were built of sterner stuff than that.

Ty wheeled Gizmo toward the warm-up ring and urged the horse into a trot. Once again, he called out apologies for his speed, but he was down to the wire.

The ring loomed closer.

One of the registrars moved to shut the gate for the next round of competitors—*his* round. He had to make it through before that gate closed or he was considered a no-show. That was *not* happening.

He spurred Gizmo forward. They sprinted for the gate, the horse's hooves pounding across the packed dirt and into the softer substrate of the ring before the registrar could respond.

"Sorry," Ty called, waving a hand in acknowledgment to the officials. He trotted over. "I had a small snafu this morning, but I made it."

"Barely," one of the men groused.

"He's here on time, William," said a woman next to him, eyeing Ty with open interest. "Leave him be. Name?"

"Tyson Covington and Doc Bar's Dippy Zippy Gizmo."

She made a note before pulling out Ty's competitor number. "Need help pinning this to your shirt?"

William snorted and pushed away from the table. "Keep your jeans on, Kathy. I'll help him."

She blushed, handing over the number.

Ty dismounted, and the man pinned the competitor's number across the shoulders of his shirt. "This'll be your number for every event you compete in. Keep it pinned to your shirt when you're on your horse for any reason." He gave Ty a friendly punch to the shoulder and stepped away. "A word of warning, though. You come through that gate at anything other than a slow trot next time, and I'll see that you're marked absent on the roster."

"That's hardly fair," Ty said as amiably as possible as he remounted Gizmo.

"I'm not so worried about fair as I am about competitors following the rules. The rules say you're here before that gate closes." He held up a hand when Ty started to protest. "Yes, you were here, but only because you ran the last hundred yards. That's not the spirit of the rule, son."

"Sir." Ty tipped his hat and spun Gizmo away, silently fuming at having been called out. What made him the angriest, though, was that the man was right.

He warmed Gizmo up with a small herd of steers. The horse seemed anxious, and Ty worked to first settle Gizmo and then himself. He tried to shake the nagging irritation of having been taken to task twice, first by his friend with benefits and second by a registrar and complete stranger. Neither sat well with him.

The announcer's voice came over the loudspeaker to announce the first competitors. Ty listened to the crowd's reaction as the first horse and rider hit their marks. The pair left the arena and their score was called shortly thereafter. Not bad, but definitely not strong enough to put the other cowboy on the boards or in the money at the end.

Ty absently listened as the next cowboy put his mount and the selected steers through their paces. He scored far better than the first rider. *A contender.*

Then it was Ty's run.

A deep breath, a swift pat to Gizmo's shoulder, then Ty reined his horse toward the arena entrance.

*Showtime.*

KENZIE FOUGHT THE urge to skip Ty's showing altogether. He'd pissed her off. More than that, he'd hurt her. It wouldn't have been such a shock if she'd expected it, but she hadn't. Not from him.

"'Entitled,' my ass," she spat, weaving her way through the crowds that were collectively pushing their way into the bleachers around the arena. She'd never been entitled. In fact, she had never been meant to be the Malone heir, and had no qualms with that particular fact. But the abrupt death of her older brother, Michael, had set her on the undesirable path that forced her to be both daughter and surrogate son to The Malone. Her father. The man who could do no wrong in the Quarter horse community.

Oh, she loved him. Wildly, in fact. He was an amazing father and friend, and most kids never experienced that rare combination. But the reality was that once she'd lost her brother, Kenzie had become the de facto heir to the Malone legacy. It wasn't something she'd ever wanted, and never, ever at that cost.

It left her trying to fill some big shoes, to live in the darkness of two shadows—Michael's, the up-and-coming rodeo star who had been the perfect older brother and ideal son, and her dad's, an infamous horseman who'd always been successful at everything he did. Kenzie wasn't perfect, and she failed as often as she succeeded. It was obvious to those around her she'd never be as good as they were.

So even insinuating she was either spoiled or entitled was the highest insult anyone could throw her way and was guaranteed a reaction. *I've earned every step forward I've taken. No one has handed me anything.*

Okay, yes. There was her trust fund. But no amount of money was worth the price she'd paid. Besides, there was certainly no dollar figure that automatically gave Ty, or anyone, the right to use words that hurt her.

If Michael were here, none of this would have happened. She wouldn't have inherited so much money, so no one would dare comment. The crushing sense of obligation to be both perfect daughter and replacement son wouldn't exist.

Three short beeps sounded. *The competition clock.* She slowed. Stopped. The crush of people worked their way around her. The first competitor was in the arena and working his, or her, group of calves. Applause followed the spectators' collective gasp.

What had happened? Curiosity ate at Kenzie. She moved with purpose toward the arena and then into the stands.

She slipped into the Malone arena-side box, bought with Malone money, respected because of the Malone name. Not hers—not yet—but her father's. He'd been a national champion in cutting, reining and roping, and his high score still stood. She'd grown up proud of him. Now? She wanted to beat him.

A small smile pulled at the corners of her lips at the same time someone opened the box and walked in, folding down the stadium seat beside her. Years in the man's presence told her who it was before she even looked into his sun-lined face. "Hey, Dad."

He slid down in his seat before draping an arm around the back of her seat. "You here to figure out a way to win or for the eye candy?"

"Dad!" The word escaped her on a rush of laughter. "You don't say things like that to your daughter."

"Hey," he exclaimed. "I'm hop. I know what's what."

"That would be 'hip,' and no, no, you don't."

He gently cuffed the back of her head. "Smart-ass."

He shifted his attention to the ring. "So who's our biggest competition this year? Still that Covington man from New Mexico? Didn't they get into some financial trouble, have to set their place up as a dude ranch to salvage it or something?"

Kenzie fought to keep her face straight. It wasn't that her dad didn't respect the hard work the Covingtons had put into saving their ranch. What bothered him was that, when he'd heard Gizmo's owner was in financial straits, Jack Malone had made a fair offer for Gizmo in an effort to help a fellow cowboy out. Even more, though, he'd wanted to get his hands on the stud horse. He hadn't taken Ty's rejection well. Of course, Ty hadn't taken the gesture as it was—at least mostly—intended, either. She'd never talked to either man about it directly, but she'd heard about it from both of them and more than once.

Her father didn't press for an answer right then, so she settled into her seat, watching the first competitor struggle to keep his calf separated from the herd. Horse and rider were out of sync. It took less time for him to lose the calf than it did for the rest of the herd to scatter. A mild round of clapping ceased when, in a fit of irritation, the rider viciously yanked the horse's head to the side and spurred him out of the arena.

Kenzie flagged down a server and asked for a program. Finding the horse and rider, she made a note regarding the horse's stall number. One benefit of having money? She could scare the man into responsible behavior with threats she could definitely follow up on. Oh… and she could buy his horse. She'd be doing both before she returned to Colorado.

Her attention shifted to the event again.

The second rider pulled a slightly above-average score, and he was clearly pleased with his performance.

That put Ty and Gizmo up next.

Kenzie took several deep breaths and blew them out with absolute control. Her dad rolled his program and slapped it against his palm repeatedly as he leaned forward to get the best view. With breakfast over, the noise level rose sharply due to the sheer volume of humanity moving in. Footfalls rumbled on the upper-level bleachers as more and more spectators filled the last vacant seats. What had been a low-level hum had grown to a near cacophony of sound. Even an experienced horse and rider could suffer from the distraction, and neither Ty nor Gizmo were accustomed to performing in indoor arenas this large. Sound seemed to echo back at both horse and rider and could fracture the focus of either. Or both.

The herd holders positioned a new group of yearlings for the incoming pair and then backed off, waiting.

At the opposite end of the arena, the gate swung open in a sweeping arc. Ty and Gizmo emerged from the dark tunnel at a lazy trot. Gizmo's head was low, the reins hanging loose. The horse seemed indifferent, almost half asleep, and Ty, with his chin to his chest, could have been napping. Their leisurely approach quieted the crowds even as it ratcheted spectator tension to a new high.

Kenzie moved to the edge of her seat. *What the hell is he thinking? The judges are going to score him down for looking so—* The buzzer sounded and she gasped.

With no visible cues from Ty, Gizmo's ears flipped forward, alert, and he started for the herd, the intent in his movements balling the cattle up. Horse and rider eased into the mass of cows and separated the first steer, peeling him away from the others with brutal efficiency. Ty and Gizmo moved in parallel harmony. The cowboy kept his hands down, his reins slack in order to give Gizmo his head. The stud horse never faltered. A whirling dervish, he spun, wheeled and darted left and right with both athleticism and showmanship that stunned not only Kenzie but the crowd, as well. She'd never seen the pair like this, had never known Ty to ride *this* professionally yet make it seem absolutely effortless.

Someone broke the silence with a whistle. Another voice shouted encouragement.

Anxiety created a solid mass between her shoulder blades. An invisible band tightened around her chest and made every breath she drew as painful as it was necessary. She wanted to scream at everyone to keep quiet, to let the pair work. If it wouldn't have generated an even larger distraction, she'd have done just that.

But Ty and Gizmo ignored every potential distraction. The horse worked the yearling and prevented his return until Ty deemed it time. Then, together, they put the animal back in the shuffling herd.

Next they sorted a much bigger steer out of the group. Obviously irritated, the steer charged the horse. Gizmo didn't give ground, instead rapidly placing himself, cross bodied, in between the steer and the herd. Confused, the steer stumbled and stopped. Gizmo took advantage of the other animal's hesitation to push him farther from the herd.

The big steer sprinted one direction, then spun and sprinted the other, trying his best to get by Gizmo. The horse wasn't having it. He met the steer's every move with a countermove that kept the animal separated from the herd.

Then on a particularly hard turn, one of Gizmo's leg splints came loose.

Kenzie's stomach dropped.

The horse ignored the support failure, charging forward to stop the steer. He slid to a stop and whirled to meet the other animal's next move.

Gizmo pushed off with his front feet, forced to make a rapid change in direction to head the steer off. The unsupported fetlock flexed and twisted in a totally unnatural manner. The cannon bone bent and the horse screamed, the sound sheer agony. The horse's momentum was unstoppable, and both Ty and Gizmo went down, the horse's right front hoof flopping sickeningly as he rolled over Ty.

Kenzie didn't think, didn't listen to her father's protests as she rose, refused to heed his restraining hand on her arm. She shrugged him off and vaulted the pipe fence, heading across the arena as fast as she could. Soft, ankle-deep dirt pulled at her feet like quicksand. The sound of her breath swamped her awareness as she pushed forward. She had to get to Ty *now.*

On some level, she was aware of onlookers shouting and the announcer's voice booming and the herd holders trying to keep the yearlings back so they didn't create more chaos. None of it mattered. What mattered was the horse groaning and unable to get up, his shredded fetlock already swelling. Even more? His rider. The man. Lord have mercy, the man...

*Tyson.*

His hat had been crushed in the fall and then flung several feet from the spot where he'd hit the dirt and gone completely still. She fixated on the hat as she ran. She knew Ty was within feet of the hat but couldn't bear to look at him too closely. One glance, one *single* glance, had dragged up memories that darkened the periphery of her consciousness, reminding her of Michael and the way he'd lain, preternaturally still in the dirt after his fall. She'd silently urged her brother to get up as he always did, to dust himself off and curse his horse and start again. But he hadn't risen. Not ever again.

*No. No, no, no!* her mind shrieked as her lungs worked harder than industrial bellows to provide her with air, to keep her moving, to keep her focused on that damned hat.

She couldn't lose someone else, couldn't watch another man she cared about die doing what he loved. She'd wouldn't recover from that a second time.

*Move, Ty. Just once. Move.*

Her heart hammered out a frantic rhythm in her chest. She stumbled, fear making her clumsy. Landing on her hands and knees, Kenzie crawled the last half-dozen yards to the unmoving man.

*No!* Her singular denial translated to a silent wail.

The closer she got, the easier it was to see he wasn't quite right. His eyes were closed, and his head… His head was canted at a strange angle. Dirt packed one ear and caked the near side of his face. And his chest failed to rise and fall.

Ty wasn't breathing.

"Please, God, no." Her broken plea was lost to the sounds of the announcer, official personnel and the crowd's frantic buzz. She ignored it all, kneeling next to him and grabbing his hand.

Ty's chest shuddered as he gasped, seizing a short breath. For ages, nothing followed. Then another short, gasped breath.

She squeezed his unresponsive fingers. "Ty? Tyson? Tyson!" she yelled, scared to touch him anywhere else even as she longed to shake him hard enough to rattle his teeth. "You answer me, damn you!"

Nothing.

"Don't you dare do this to me," she whispered. The harsh words brimmed with anger, demand and fear.

Sirens chirped and forced her to look up. The ambulance and EMTs were headed their way. The vet's emergency truck and flatbed trailer followed.

*Gizmo...*

Still gripping his hand, she leaned forward. "You fight, Covington. *You. Fight.*"

His fingers spasmed against her hand. One booted foot flopped to the side only to lie perfectly still again. Then his eyelids fluttered. The deep mink of his irises showed for a split second before his eyes slipped closed.

"You stubborn man! Gizmo needs you. Wake up and deal with this catastrophe. I'm not cleaning up after you. Do you hear me?" she demanded. Hysteria's sharp claws scrabbled their way up her spine as the seconds passed and he didn't answer. "Tyson!" She squeezed his hand hard enough to grind the bones together.

His fingertips pressed into her hand, the movement faint but undeniable.

A man and woman raced up to her, and she recognized Cade Covington before he skidded to a stop. Eyes wide, he fixated on Ty, and when he spoke, his deep voice trembled. "Tyson." He grabbed his female companion's hand, uttered a pained sound and then pulled her against his body.

She wordlessly folded into him, her eyes fixed on Ty and brimming with tears.

The ambulance stopped a few feet away, and two EMTs hopped out. One grabbed a body board as the other, already gloved up, approached. He crowded her out, the act far from gentle. "I need you to leave the ring, ma'am."

"Like hell," she snarled. She had to stay, couldn't leave him, not like this. *Wouldn't* leave him. "He's mine." The lie emerged without conscious thought.

The man shot her a sharp look even as he pulled on blue nitrile gloves. "Your husband?"

She didn't even hesitate. "He's. Mine."

He scrutinized her before lifting one shoulder and getting to work. "Fine, but stay out of my way."

Cade stared at her, skepticism filtering through his initial shock at her declaration.

She ignored him, ignored everyone but Ty and the EMT. Terror wove its way around her heart and up her throat, stopping just shy of spilling out her mouth on a keening wail. Focusing on the EMT, she managed to rasp out a desperate "Help him."

She heard raised voices behind her. Eli Covington and a woman she assumed was his new wife stood with rodeo vet. The three of them were arguing as Gizmo lay there, his sides heaving, hide slicked with sweat.

"The animal is in pain," the vet said. "Putting him down would be the humane thing."

"I'm about to hit you so hard your dentist won't need to worry about which teeth to keep. I guarantee that'll result in pain. Yours." The woman, tall enough to look at the man eye to eye, stepped close enough to invade his personal space. "You suggesting I put you down then, too? As a matter of 'humane' treatment?"

"That's different," the man objected. "I'm human."

She pointed at Ty's still form. "You euthanize this horse, you might as well put him down, too, because you'll destroy him and everything he's worked for."

Eli said something low to his wife.

She rounded on him. "Don't you dare tell me not to get worked up! I don't care if I'm six weeks' or six months' pregnant. Neither my hormones nor the baby responsible for them changes right and wrong."

Ty squeezed Kenzie's hand again, stronger this time but still far weaker than he should have been capable of. His eyelids fluttered before he ground his teeth and opened unfocused eyes. "Save…"

"We're working on saving you, Mr. Covington." The EMT scowled. "You've got to be still, though. We have to establish how much damage the accident caused your cervical spine."

"Screw spine," he whispered brokenly. His pain-filled gaze roamed wildly, skipping over her face and coming back. He fought to focus. "Giz… Save…" Tears rolled down his temples, and he squeezed her hand harder. "Please, Kenzie."

"I'll do what I can," she answered, voice husky.

"No." His tears flowed faster. "Promise."

"You have to calm down, Mr. Covington." The EMT pulled a syringe and loaded it. "I'm going to give you something for the pain before we transport you."

"Promise!" he rasped, grasping Kenzie's hand hard.

"I promise," she choked out, but his eyes had already drifted closed, and she had no idea if he'd heard her before the drug hit.

His hand relaxed. She clung to him, unwilling to let him go.

"Where are you taking him?" she asked, standing as they lifted the body board.

"Medevacing him to Baylor's trauma center."

Kenzie looked at Cade. "Go with him. I'll check in later after I take care of Gizmo."

"Take care of him how?" Cade demanded.

"Don't worry, I have a vested interest in ensuring the horse survives."

Cade's fiancée narrowed her eyes. "Ty didn't mention anyone else having a vested interest in Gizmo."

"Have you talked to Ty about his business dealings since he's been here?" Kenzie asked with feigned arrogance.

Cade arched a single brow. "No."

"Then, I don't expect you to know that I bought into the horse here or that I'm funding part of your brother's breeding program." Any other time it would have bothered her how easily she lied. Not right now, though. Too much was at stake. "I won't let my investment fall apart."

"Gotta go, folks," the EMT called.

"Do what you can," the short-haired woman said, grabbing Cade's hand and hauling him toward the ambulance. They hopped inside, the ambulance driver slamming the door closed behind them before racing for the driver's seat. The ambulanced chirped and, with lights flashing, took off.

Kenzie turned to the rodeo vet. "What's the prognosis?"

"Unless you own the horse—"

"I have a vested interest, yes." *How many lies would a cowgirl issue if a cowgirl could issue lies?* The answer was simple: as many as it took. "Let's consider the broken parts mine, so tell me what I'm facing here."

"He's torn ligaments and tendons in his fetlock, and I'm going to wager he's also fractured his cannon. We've got a Kimzey leg saver on its way, but the damage…"

He shrugged. "He'll require serious surgical intervention. If he's worth anything at all, get him to Ohio State University."

Eli's wife paled. "You're talking thousands just in transport."

"Make it happen," Kenzie said, crossing her arms and widening her stance.

The vet arched a brow. "You realize that between emergency transport and initial treatment you're looking at fifty to eighty thousand dollars?"

"You signing the checks?" she asked quietly.

"No."

"Then, don't worry about the costs."

"We have to, though," Eli murmured.

Kenzie shook her head. "No, you don't." Facing the vet again, she tucked her hands into her jeans pockets and did the one thing she hated doing. She threw her name at the doctor with the force of a major league pitcher's fastball. "I'm Mackenzie Malone, Jack Malone's daughter." The vet's eyes widened and he opened his mouth to say something, but Kenzie shook her head. "There are only two things I want to hear from you. First, I want this horse's flight number to the airport nearest Ohio State University. Charter a plane if necessary. Second, I want the in-flight pain management plans for him so I can clear that plan with my own vet."

The rodeo vet stiffened. "I assure you—"

"I listed the two things I need, Doc, and your assurances weren't on the short list." Dismissing him to do his job as she'd seen her father do a thousand times, she faced the Covingtons. "Ty's being lifted to Baylor. You two go there. I'll stay with Gizmo."

"Don't let them put him down. Please, Ms. Malone."

Eli choked on the words and looked away, but not fast enough to hide the sheen of tears in his eyes.

"Just Kenzie, and I give you my word I'll do my best to avoid that very thing, Mr. Covington."

The woman pulled out her admission ticket and grabbed a pen from a vet tech. She scribbled on the back, then handed the card to Kenzie. "I'm Reagan Covington, large-animal vet and Eli's wife. Call me with the drug names and I can explain what they're giving him."

"Will do. Now you two go on. Ty needs you, and frankly, I can make things happen faster if I have a little room to play the bitchy heiress."

Both Covington and his wife issued their thanks before jogging toward the nearest arena exit.

Kenzie went to her knees by Gizmo's head. She stroked his jaw and murmured soft words of encouragement. It took her several moments to summon the courage to meet his gaze. When she did, her heart broke for him. His nostrils blew hard, froth decorated his lips and neck, and the whites of his eyes showed clearly. He hurt. Worse than the pain, though, was his obvious fear. It was as if he had some inkling of just how bad off he was, and he was terrified.

That made two of them.

# 4

KENZIE KNEW THE exact moment her dad entered the fray. Things started to happen at twice their normal speed. The vet became respectful versus argumentative, and that—*that*—pissed Kenzie off more than anything. As a petite woman dominating the leaderboards in a man's sport, she had to earn every iota of respect she received. Carrying the Malone name only made it more difficult. There were always the behind-the-back allegations that she'd never have made it this far if it hadn't been for her father. For all that it was bull, the quiet whispers stung. The song "Should've Been a Cowboy" by Toby Keith rang true. Neither the title nor the lyrics said it was a blessing to be a cow*girl*. She wouldn't allow them to push her aside because she was female.

Shoving her way through to the vet, she stepped up beside her father and shot him a hard glance through dark lashes. "I'll manage this, Dad."

"Seemed to me you could use a little help."

"Nope. He—" she jabbed a finger in the vet's direction "—will do better when he learns a little respect for women and a hell of a lot *more* respect for animals."

"There're better ways to get what you want, Mackenzie."

"Well, right now Gizmo's down, so tossing the last name around will have to do." Rounding on the very man under discussion, she ignored the people milling about, the weight of the crowd's collective stare and, above all, she fought to keep her attention off the pain poor Gizmo was suffering. He had to come first. She focused on the one man who could truly help him. "Dose him with dermorphin so we can get him in a hoist and moved."

"I need proof you have authority over the animal, ma'am, because he's registered under Tyson Covington's name."

"I already explained this. I bought into him prior to the accident." She didn't think twice about uttering the lie again. Not until she realized her father had overheard.

"Excuse us for a second." He took her by the arm and led her a few steps away. Jack Malone's eyes were bright, glittering with a type of predatory anticipation she'd never seen outside competition. "I've been trying to get Covington to sell me half rights to Gizmo for over three years. How did you manage it?"

"Feminine wiles?" A question and not a declarative statement. Guilt tightened her throat, the sensation spreading to her chest. She'd always been honest with her dad. She'd been his shadow as long as she could remember. How could she lie to him, particularly about something he wanted so badly? Easy. She couldn't. Opening her mouth to admit her deception, he plowed forward in excitement.

"I'll have Alyssa make arrangements to get this horse to Ohio State and the Galbreath Equine Center's emergency medicine team." He pulled his cell and called his barn manager. "Alyssa, I need you to charter a flight for an injured horse—Fort Worth to the nearest airport to the Galbreath Center." He paused then shook his head. "No, not Indie. Kenzie managed to buy into Covington's Dippy Zippy Gizmo just before the stud was injured." Another pause. "I have no idea how she managed to do it. We'll get details later. Right now, that horse has to get on his way. I'll have Kenzie book the next flight to Columbus since she should be on the ground before the horse in order to receive him. Tell the Center to do whatever is necessary to save this animal. Cost isn't an issue. I'll call you back shortly. Thanks, Alyssa."

Kenzie wanted to puke. The lie had taken on a life of its own and was about to cost her father a hell of a lot of money. She couldn't live with this, couldn't let him foot the bill and then find out the truth. "Dad, maybe you shouldn't do this. I don't actually—"

"Honey, it's all right. I trust you implicitly. You'll be my eyes and ears, acting in my stead to make sure this horse gets the best of everything." He pulled her into a bear hug. "I'm so glad we're finally partnering with the Covingtons and have the means to help save this magnificent animal."

Guilt hung in her throat, both bitter and sour. "I haven't been—"

"I know you haven't ridden yet, Kenzie, but don't worry, honey. You're amazing on horseback and you're young still. There'll be more opportunities for you to chase my record. I'm proud as hell that you're putting others' well-being in front of your own success." He stepped away and grasped her shoulders before meeting her gaze. "Call me with your flight details." His attention drifted to the horse, who lay in the soft arena dirt, sides heaving, one front fetlock terribly swollen and distorted in a macabre, stomach-churning manner. "You remind me so much of Michael, thinking on your feet like this."

She'd lived to ease her parents' pain after Michael's death, worked her ass off to be good enough at everything she did to make them proud, and here she was, hearing the words for the first time.

The irony wasn't lost on her. Jack Malone, known for his honesty and straightforward talk, wasn't *proud* of her based on her own merit. It had taken things beyond her control and one whopping lie to hear the words she'd longed for from him.

Sure in the knowledge she was dooming herself by letting the truth stay buried, she hugged him hard before starting for the end of the arena where the golf carts were kept. She got a driver to return her to her hotel, stuffed all her belongings into her suitcase and less than forty minutes later was in a hired car bound for the airport.

She dug out her cell phone, pulled up the internet and paused. If she called her dad now, she could come clean, tell him she'd pay for the horse's care from her trust fund. She wouldn't have to live with the immense burden so many lies created.

She closed the web browser and pulled up her dad's cell number.

Her thumb hovered over the call button.

*I trust you implicitly.*

*I'm proud as hell that you're doing the right thing.*

*You remind me so much of Michael.*

Confessing now would destroy his pride in her, would make him regret losing Michael all the more because her brother never would have backed himself into a corner like this.

"Way to go, Mackenzie," she muttered, closing the phone function on her smartphone and returning to the web browser.

It only took a few taps of the screen on the airline's booking page to have her seated in 3A on the next flight to Columbus, Ohio.

Kenzie dropped her phone in her messenger bag, then settled back into the seat. The image of Ty's broken body flashed through her mind. She shivered.

There was more to this than just her father's pride in her. At least part of the reason she was going through with this was the sheer terror she'd witnessed in Ty's eyes. She'd felt an emotional connection with him, a shared purpose that bound them together in this. She could save him, save his horse, where she'd failed Michael that day. Now she might set the past to rights by saving Gizmo, and in turn, giving Ty a reason to fight harder to recover, to live.

And she needed him to live. In the privacy of the backseat of the car, she could admit she cared about him. Cared far more than was wise, no doubt.

But for a split second when she'd first approached Tyson after the accident…

His chest hadn't moved.

Hers had stopped in kind.

He'd had no pulse.

Hers had stalled without even an indignant sputter.

His eyes hadn't fluttered.

She'd been unable to blink.

He'd been as still as death.

And a part of her had died.

The thought alone was enough to make her throw herself into Gizmo's well-being. Being near the horse would put her near Ty, and it would give her time to work out how to handle her dad. And she could avoid looking too closely, or even at all, at the complicated emotional chaos she'd faced when, for that split second, she'd thought she'd lost Ty forever.

TY KNEW THINGS WERE, at best, pretty damn bad. If someone would've taken the time to explain just *how* bad, he'd have appreciated it. Chances were good they assumed he couldn't hear them, though. Seeing as he couldn't currently force his eyes open, it was a fair assumption. But it was still wrong. During the many moments of dark lucidity, he heard every word.

As it was, the best he could do was focus on squeezing his hands or flexing his feet when instructed. No matter how miserably he knew he'd failed, strangers' voices praised him. Now and again he'd hear a voice he recognized. That was when he'd fight hardest to open his eyes. The effort always proved too much, but it wasn't enough to take the fight out of him. He needed to know what had happened, needed to see the truth in the faces around him. Those faces wouldn't lie to him.

Yet no matter how hard he fought against the pain that enveloped his brief battles to remain conscious, he continued to surface to darkness and descend into darkness.

So he listened.

And heard the same phrases over and over.

"Cervical involvement at C2 and C3."

"Neurological impairment unknown."

"Long-term prognosis undetermined."

"Lucky to be alive."

He was aware he lost blocks of time, but was sure that time had passed because the voices of his caregivers changed. Day and night ceased to exist. The hum of machines and the squeeze and flex commands from those voices became his only constant.

That was why it surprised him when he finally rose from the darkness and found the room blindingly bright. He opened his mouth and a very feminine sob escaped. More confused than ever, he closed his mouth, but the sobbing continued.

Not him, then.

He blinked slowly. When he forced his eyes open again, a woman with a penlight hovered over him. She lifted first one eyelid and then the other, flashing the light in his eyes. The beam pierced his skull as wave after wave of nausea rolled through him.

"Uh," Ty managed to grunt in protest.

"Glad to hear you're finally protesting all the poking and prodding," she said on a smile. "Can you manage to squeeze my fingers, Tyson?"

Concentrating, he squeezed as hard as he could.

"That's good. Better than yesterday."

Her comment, couched in cheerful enthusiasm, didn't fool him one bit. He was weak as an abandoned calf in mid-January. Hopefully his chances of survival were better.

He blanked out again. When he opened his eyes, the sobbing was softer, removed from him somehow, and two male faces loomed over him. Ty tried to raise his hand, but it seemed heavier than a concrete footer. Licking his lips, he tried to nod his chin. No go.

*Will nothing move?*

Machines beeped with mechanical urgency, reflecting his rising panic. The hushed *whoosh*-pause, *whoosh*-pause of a ventilator made him want to choke on the tube down his throat. Eyes wide, he was ashamed at the tears that trailed down his temples as his panicked gaze sought those of his brothers'. He managed to raise the first finger on his right hand. A nurse rushed into the room.

She went to a monitor just outside his field of vision and murmured, "Tyson, honey, you have to calm down," as she manipulated the machine and made the incessant *beep-beep-beep*ing stop. Fishing around in her pocket, she pulled something free.

Ty strained to see what she'd come up with. It wasn't by sight that recognition hit but instead by the lethargic weight that stole over him and began to pull heavily on his consciousness.

*Damn if she didn't sedate me when I just woke* up.

He was frantic to stay awake, but it took only seconds for his vision to blur and his brothers to become optical twins—two of Cade, two of Eli.

The soft sound of feminine tears stopped.

"Rest, Ty." Cade's voice was rough, as if it hadn't been used in ages.

"We'll be here when you wake up," Eli added, reaching down to grip Ty's hand.

He'd have felt a whole lot better if he'd been able to grip that hand back. Then the pharmaceutical cocktail hit and took him down before he even registered the count.

TKO.

# 5

IT HAD BEEN almost seven weeks since Mackenzie arrived in Ohio with Gizmo, and there were two things she knew with relative certainty. First, the horse couldn't have had better care. Second, January was the worst possible month to visit Ohio.

She tugged the neckline of her jacket higher and blinked rapidly, the wind freezing her eyes and burning her chapped lips as she rounded the corner of the building and sped up in her effort to reach the heated barn.

Inside, Kenzie went straight to Gizmo, pulled her hands out of her pockets and slipped the big guy a couple of sugar cubes. She slowly rubbed his face, jaw to muzzle and back, and murmured to him as the vet, Dr. Trey Harris, removed the vet wrap and nonstick pads that covered the surgical sites. The pins had come out and the horse was bearing weight regularly, yet for all that, his foot still looked like something from a horror flick. The incisions were healing fine, but there were still angry welts where the surgical pins had been inserted in both his fetlock and pastern, and all around the last of the sutures the skin was raw and red. The swelling had abated, though. Enough so she could see Gizmo's improvement. Still, the idea of the pain he'd endured— still endured—made her throat tight.

"When—" The one word came out scratchy, so she forced herself to slow down and breathe before facing the vet. "When can the big guy go home?"

Dr. Harris glanced up at her and one corner of his mouth curled up in a slow, lazy smile. "You getting tired of staring at my pretty face?"

Laughing, Kenzie shook her head. "You're easy on the eyes but you're not a cheap date, Dr. Harris." She sighed dramatically. "I just don't see a long-term future for us."

The vet, easily her father's age or older, chuckled, never ceasing his ministrations to the leg and ankle he'd essentially rebuilt the day Gizmo, and she, had arrived. He didn't answer her, though.

So she pressed. "I was hoping to move his care to the ranch before the end of the month. Is that reasonable?"

"What kind of care do you have in place for him at home?"

"The barn is clean and dry but certainly not a sterile environment. However, I can have a cement pad laid for him and rubber nonslip floor tiles installed. And once I have a return date, I'll arrange a sling and will incorporate whatever physical therapies you recommend. I can have my vet fly in to check on him, and Ty's sister-in-law is a large-animal vet, too. Then there's you." She batted her eyes at him. "I don't suppose you'd make a couple, maybe three…or four, house calls, would you?"

"I'm available." He fluttered his lashes at her and

made fish lips. "But like you said earlier, I'm an expensive prospect."

"Only the best for this guy." She patted Gizmo's neck.

Dr. Harris sobered. "I'm serious. It would be pretty costly to buy my time in such large chunks because I'd have to bill you for the hours away from the clinic."

"Sure, but leaving him here long-term can't be much, if any, cheaper. Along with vet bills, I have to consider feed, board, grooming and his handler's fees, as well as my own room, board and rental car. It all adds up fast. Flying you in to visit him would, by all accounts, be more reasonable."

"True. I just want you to understand there will be additional costs to having me examine him on site, and those visits will occur subject to my availability."

"If the horse needs it, trust that I'll do it."

"Fair enough." He paused when he hit a sensitive spot and the horse twitched and then pawed the air as passively as a 1,200-pound animal could. "So whose barn should we make arrangements to deliver him to?

Kenzie jerked upright, stiff as a board. "The Covington barn. Why?"

"Just wondered whose home he was going to since your dad and Covington are equal partners now."

Her brow furrowed. "Who said my dad was an equal partner?"

"That would be—" he gestured toward her "—*your dad.*"

"If there's a partner in this, it isn't Jack Malone." Her shoulders sagged a fraction. "It's me."

"You don't seem happy about that."

"It's complicated." She didn't offer any more because there wasn't more to say. That and she didn't want to start any rumors. When Dr. Harris opened his mouth, she cut him off with a sharp shake of her head. "Let's leave it at 'complicated.' How soon can I get him home?"

The vet worked his fingers down Gizmo's leg, along the cannon bone that had been fractured in the accident. "I'm admittedly pleased with how clean he's healed." Standing, he brushed off his hands and then shoved them into his coat pockets, considering her. "Let me finish up here, get a new set of X-rays and we'll talk dates. I'm guessing you'll hang around until I'm through?"

*Don't I always?* "Sure." The metal cribbing rail on the stall delivered a shock of cold when her jacket sleeves slipped up as she leaned forward to rest her arms on the door. Sure, Colorado was cold, but it wasn't as cold as this. There was snow in Colorado, but that meant ski season opened, not that the snowbirds fled south.

*South.*

She was far more snow bunny than bird, but she'd be heading south with Gizmo. That meant she'd be facing off with Ty sooner rather than later. Her stomach did this weird gymnastics routine. If the vet up here had heard about the "partnership" she'd asserted where Gizmo was concerned, it was safe to assume Ty had heard the same. Though that was pure speculation, seeing as she hadn't talked to him. Not yet. Kenzie had limited all correspondence to email exchanges with Reagan. Her logic had been simple: by limiting her emails to Reagan, and *only* Reagan, Kenzie didn't have to worry about what she'd said to whom and when she'd said it. There were fewer chances she'd have to stretch the truth in different directions to better support the tales she'd already told.

Except with her dad. She'd tried to clear that up.

Man, she'd tried. But every time she brought up the horse's progress, her dad always launched into some grand speech about how proud of her he was and how she was doing the right thing by both families, helping the Covingtons pay medical bills they'd never have been able to afford all while praising her for "this great new partnership that's getting the Covington boy's superior genetics program integrated into our herd." How was she supposed to tell him the whole thing was a sham she'd cooked up in a split second because she hadn't wanted to be separated from her prime competitor who was, by the way, her lover? That was bound to go over well.

And how was she supposed to tell him she was spending Malone money on a horse their family had no rights to? Most of all, how was she supposed to tell her dad she'd lied to him, to everyone, and that she was nothing at all like Michael? She was never meant for this, to be son and daughter, sole heir and youngest child.

"I can't," she whispered, the two-word admission carried away by the howling winds outside.

"I'll make arrangements to have the horse cleared for travel in roughly two weeks, provided you agree to follow my instructions for his recovery and therapy."

Shoving her hands into her pockets, she forced her spiraling thoughts to step aside, giving her whole attention to the doctor. "Two weeks?"

"At the outside, yes." The vet glanced at Gizmo's front foot. "Swim therapy would really help him strengthen that joint and encourage faster strengthening of the muscles and tendons that support his front end." Dr. Harris pulled his toque off and scrubbed one hand through his short hair. The effect left him looking like he'd uncovered an irritated hedgehog.

Kenzie grinned. "I'll have a pool installed."

"Of course you will," the vet said with an answering smile. "And stop laughing at my hair."

"Can't," she admitted, her grin widening. "You've been hiding a hedgehog under your hat the entire time. It's as if suddenly you're not the man I thought you were."

He gave her a mock dirty look. "My wife says the same thing."

Kenzie couldn't control her laughter. "Smart woman," she said between peals.

"Get out of my barn, kid," the older man groused good-naturedly. "I've got to get this guy ready to go."

She sobered enough to add, "I'll make sure your aftercare plan is followed to a T."

He nodded. "Go ahead and book his flight for the first of February. I'll have him ready by then. You ready to take this on?"

Her thoughts scattered like dandelion fuzz in the face of a hopeful child's breath. She could get the horse home, arrange to have his therapy taken care of and see Gizmo emerge as strong as he would ever be. But the horse wasn't the only factor. The Covingtons would expect answers. Her dad would expect results from a partnership that didn't exist.

And Ty? She shouldn't have anything to worry about. She'd done what she had to do in order to ensure his wishes were carried out. Facing him would be hard, admitting she'd lied to save Gizmo even harder. But she'd do it without apologizing.

She shifted her gaze to the horse, reaching out to

straighten his forelock. "I guess there isn't any other option, is there?"

And that was the hell of it.

There wasn't.

# 6

SOMEONE HAD ARRANGED the furniture to create what Ty called his "parking space" in front of the big picture window in the main house's living room. He sat there far too often, looking out over the little bit of ranch the view afforded. To the east, he watched as one of the hired hands crested the hill on horseback, bringing in the newest group of guests from their first trail ride. The horses all looked good. Ty would have to thank Cade for making that a priority despite all his other responsibilities. Not that his brother wouldn't have done it on his own, but Ty knew the horses were being paraded for his approval. Probably to make him feel like he was part of things. But he wasn't. Not anymore. The cowboy never would have brought them so close to the house otherwise.

A sigh escaped him, sounding far too close to self-pity for his comfort. Provided he was careful, didn't reinjure his neck and did all his physical therapy, his disabilities were temporary. Knowing that wasn't enough to curb his frustrations, though. Or his fears. Never in a million years had he thought his life would end up like this. He'd been arrogant. Vain. Assumed himself invincible. Now he rode an electric wheelchair instead of his horse.

*Gizmo.*

The stud horse would be home today, arriving three days after Ty had. He was anxious, scared to see the horse who was more than just "an animal" to him, afraid Gizmo had suffered more than Ty had imagined. And imagine he had. He'd thought of Gizmo a thousand times every day. He'd created the worst-case scenarios over and over as he tried to spur his memory to recall the details of the fall. Sure, his family had discussed the accident with him, but he'd chosen not to watch the replay on the DVR. There was no doubt in anyone's mind, least of all his own, that he'd take it hard. Still, if things had been as horrible as he imagined, the horse wouldn't have come through with the positive reports from the vet. And *only* the vet.

Not once had Kenzie called him. Not once had she reached out to let him know how Gizmo was recovering or talk about this mysterious agreement that had been forged between them. Pride kept him from admitting to his family that he had no recollection of the agreement. He hadn't wanted Gizmo's care interrupted. Selfish? Yes. That didn't change the truth behind his choice, though.

He wasn't stupid. There was no way he, or the ranch, could have afforded to cover the costs of the Galbreath center. So he'd kept quiet, fighting to remember what he'd agreed to. The one thing he knew? Whatever agreement they'd struck had been after the accident, because he recalled with great clarity everything that had happened before he'd gone into the arena. Ty resented her for preying on his weakness and her choice not to communicate with him. Sure, she'd been emailing Reagan as the veterinarian who'd take over Gizmo's rehab when he came home. Reagan had relayed the messages.

But Kenzie hadn't called anyone, hadn't reached out to *him* at all. She had to know how bad he wanted the information. She understood what this horse meant to him, probably better than anyone. She understood what losing Gizmo would do to his breeding program, to *him*. Why? Because she understood him. Or so he'd thought. Seemed he'd misjudged her character. Badly.

A dust cloud rose from the road that led into the ranch from the south. A horse hauler rounded the slight bend in the drive. The sun gleamed off its bright white-and-chrome exterior. Ty squinted. Behind the hauler came a fancy truck-and-trailer combo he didn't recognize.

"Someone's here," he called through the house, doing his best to ignore the faint bitterness in his words. Before, he'd have slapped his hat on and headed out to meet the truck. Now? He'd been reduced to reporting the goings-on. Nothing more.

Heavy footsteps were followed by lighter, decidedly feminine ones. "Who is it?" his sister-in-law Reagan asked as she peered over his shoulder.

"Fancy setup," his eldest brother and Reagan's husband, Eli, commented. "Has to be Gizmo. I can't imagine him arriving in anything less with a Malone arranging his travel."

Reagan laid a hand on Ty's shoulder and glanced back at Eli. "Says the man who lived alone in a six-thousand-square-foot house."

Ty forced a smile. "Make sure they put him in the first stall past the tack room, would you?"

"Sure." Reagan slipped her sunglasses on and headed

for the door. "Might be handy to have the attorney around if there are forms to sign."

Eli's voice drifted back to Ty as he followed his wife. "Is that all I am—your legal monkey?"

"Just be grateful I haven't sold you to a traveling circus."

Ty listened as the front door closed and muffled their voices. He wheeled his chair from the window so he faced away from the scene outside. He envied them the sunshine on their shoulders, the breeze in their faces and open air around them. The ability to walk without limitations or fear of falling. To ride out across the pasture. To see the new foals that had arrived in his absence. Those little ones wouldn't know him, would consider him an unidentified threat, and that sickened him. He'd never missed the birth of a foal, never missed the chance to rub them down and be there every day thereafter. Now? It would be ages before he could get to the barn, get involved, get to know the babies.

"Hello, Ty."

The feminine voice startled him. He'd been so lost in thought he hadn't heard anyone enter. He spun the chair toward the intruder. Recognition was as effective as a punch to the gut. "Mackenzie Malone. Couldn't spare a call, huh? So why are you here now? Come to check out the crippled cowboy? Or did you come in to write a check in the hopes you'd buy some goodwill? I expected better of you."

Her cheeks paled and she reacted as if shoved, taking a step back before recovering. "Feeling's mutual." She lifted her chin a notch, her eyes narrowing. "And I didn't come into the house to buy anything. I was there, in Texas, when you were hurt. Unfortunately, no one bothered to tell me your attitude was maimed along with everything else." Kenzie stepped closer and propped a hip on the sofa arm, one leg slowly kicking back and forth as the other one held her in place. "I didn't immediately announce myself because you were brooding. I thought I'd let you get it out of your system. Looks as if that isn't happening, so brood away."

"You didn't spend two weeks in a coma. You didn't nearly lose your life on national television. Both your legs work just fine. Riding is a joy you indulge in and take for granted every day. So don't you come in here and judge me, Mackenzie." There was a world of accusation in his words, a world he hadn't intended to tap into. "Go back to your gilded castle and play at breeding quality horses. You have no right to be part of this, no right to be here."

She stiffened, her eyes widening before she schooled the emotions chasing one after another across her face. "Don't have the right?" Her lips thinned. "I beg to differ."

"Begging's a good place to start, sweetheart." Ty leaned against the wheelchair's armrest to catch every single word, every expression, anxious to have it out with the woman who'd run off with his horse the first chance she had. The same woman who had forgotten him as soon as she'd taken what she wanted, and it hadn't been him. It surprised him how much that stung, but damn if he'd admit it. He curled one lip up in a half smile, half snarl. "Go on, then. I'm waiting."

Her eyes narrowed to finite slits, blue irises sparking wildly. "I'm sorry?"

"That's the way. Is this the first time you've ever groveled? Keep it up. You'll get the hang of it."

She opened her mouth only to snap it shut and stare at him. Seconds passed before she spoke again. "What's your damage, Covington?"

"Are you *blind*?" he half shouted. "My problem is I'm *sitting*, Malone, and it's not because I'm lazy. I'm here, stuck in this damn house, watching as some stranger delivers my horse—*my horse*—and parks him in a stall in heaven only knows *what* condition!" Yep. Full-on shouting now. He wasn't proud, but he wasn't going to apologize. She had it coming, keeping information on Gizmo sequestered the way she had. He'd understood the horse was getting the best care possible, but nothing in life was free. At some point, she'd want something in return.

Crossing her arms, she stood.

"Lording it over me, huh?" he continued. "That you can stand and I can't? Feel good to finally be able to beat me at something?"

Her lips all but disappeared in that beautiful face. "Of all the people outside your immediate circle, I'm most aware you were as injured as Gizmo. But don't you dare, *dare*, throw down the verbal gauntlet unless you're prepared to take the gloves off, too."

"I had a right to know about my horse, to see him settled today!"

"Like hell you did!" she shouted in return. "You're in no condition to handle that horse right now. You'd despair, and he'd know. He's a sensitive animal. He has to focus on getting through physical therapy, very much like you do. He deserves every chance to make as full a recovery as is physically possible, or everything that's gone into saving him was wasted. Same goes for you. There's a pattern here, in case you're not seeing it. Fifty bucks says you're yelling at me because you're making asinine assumptions about how I pity you, sitting in the house in the wheelchair." She sucked in a breath and blew it out on a harsh exhale before pushing forward. "Do the responsible thing for once in your life and put someone else's needs in front of your own. Don't go see Gizmo until you can keep from treating him as if he's crippled. And do yourself a favor. Stop forcing everyone else to regard you, and treat you, the same way."

Every bit of heat drained from his face as Ty listened to her accusations. He nodded, fighting to swallow the emotion clogging his throat.

She stepped forward and loomed over him.

The move forced him to roll his eyes up to see her. "Step away, would you?" he bit out.

"Move your chair."

"You coldhearted—"

"Don't you dare finish that sentence." One degree further and the ice in her voice would have rimed the windows. "I know you've been handed a raw deal, but don't let yourself be reduced by circumstance to calling a woman foul names. You're a better man than that. Or you were." He started to defend himself, but she waved a hand between them and spoke over him, drowning out any defense he might have delivered. "I'm exhausted, I haven't been home in two months and I missed my chance at nationals because I was playing nursemaid. You owe me courtesy—no, you owe me bone-deep *gratitude*." Blue eyes sparked wildly as heat climbed her cheeks. "I'm not willing to negotiate on that. Like it or not, you owe me."

He closed his eyes and blindly steered his chair away from her. They both knew she'd taken the gloves off with that last comment.

Tyson Covington rarely owed anyone, and when he did? He always paid up.

Always.

KENZIE STORMED OUT of the house, a sticky miasma of dark emotion roiling through her. Fear. Heartache. Frustration. Compassion. Fury. There were more—so many more—but none she'd ever thought she'd have to deal with in relation to Ty Covington.

*Liar.*

"Damn it, Mackenzie Malone, you knew what you were getting into with this." The impact of her cowboy boots on hard earth punctuated each step. Yanking her ball cap off her head, she slapped it against one leg in time with her stride as she headed to the barn with new purpose.

She wouldn't walk away from Gizmo. She'd known him since he'd started traveling with Ty as a yearling to get used to shows. She'd watched him from his first performance. From day one, he'd been magnificent. One of the worst moments of her life had been looking into his pain-filled eyes that seemed to plead with her for salvation. Any salvation.

She usually harbored incredible guilt about using her trust fund—guilt that half that money used to belong to a brother she'd cherished. Guilt that all the money in the world couldn't bring him back.

Not this time. This time the money had managed to save someone.

But for all she'd operated on the belief she'd done right by Gizmo and Ty, the man had proved in a matter of minutes that this thing between them—this debt incurred, this debt owed—would stand between them.

The thing that made her angriest was that he had jumped all over her for doing the very things he'd asked her to do. How could she ever win against someone who asked for an immense favor and then punished her for giving him what he'd asked for?

No, she hadn't called him. There was a reason, though—a reason she wasn't ready to face, let alone own.

Pausing, she leaned against the shiny trailer, shocked by the cold when she touched her forehead to the metal. "Take your own advice and suck it up." Wide-open space swallowed her quiet words, protecting her from being overheard.

*Okay, fine. I'll deal with the truth.* She'd known Ty would have trouble talking around the neck brace. That he wouldn't be able to cope with verbal updates on Gizmo's condition, particularly when it had been iffy whether the horse would ever walk again.

She thumped her head against the trailer. "Chicken-shit." Louder than her last admission, but the harsh accusation was still for her ears alone.

*Truth, then*, she thought. *Real, hard truth.* She'd known she'd be returning Gizmo to the Covington ranch. She'd see her commitment through to the end. She didn't shirk her duties or shy away from the hard stuff when it came down to brass tacks. But she hadn't been sure she could face Ty's condition. He would walk again, but no one knew how well. And ride? That was up in the air at the moment. And ride Gizmo? That was so far in the future that the calendar hadn't even been printed yet.

"Truth," she said again, the self-command a rough one. It was all these things and more that scared her, but seeing Ty broken had been enough to nearly drop her to her knees.

The vibrancy of the man had been diminished by both circumstance and the reality he now faced. She could see it in his face, that knowledge. That moment when she'd stepped into the house, that moment when she simply observed the near hopeless desperation on his face, had ripped her heart out. When he'd rounded on her, she hadn't blamed him. Not one bit. But pride wouldn't let her take poor treatment from him, either. She was in over her head where that man was concerned.

She'd spent the past two months lost in a world of probabilities and survival statistics. She hadn't applied those to the man who meant so much to her. At least, not until she saw him. Now? The idea that he might not ever be 100 percent again made her want to scream at the heavens over the injustice.

"You look as though you could use this."

Kenzie spun around so abruptly she knocked the ceramic mug out of the redhead's hand. Rich, dark coffee splashed out in flash-frame movement, the cup tumbling to the ground and shattering.

"Sorry." The redhead rushed forward. "I'm so sorry. I didn't mean to crowd you at all. I was only trying to get out of this blasted wind—"

"It's all good," Kenzie said, interrupting. "I promise. I was just—"

A dark-haired woman stepped up to join them. "I hope you're going to finish that sentence with 'going to see if Gizmo was settled.' I swear, the big guy's moping without Ty."

On cue, a horse's bugle cut across the wind that whipped across the plains. The sound would undoubtedly carry to the house, and Ty would cringe. It would hurt him to hear the horse calling for him when he was unable to get down to the barn.

*What if I was wrong earlier? What if the best thing for Gizmo is to see Ty? And if Ty witnesses the proof of Gizmo's improvement, maybe he'll want to be part of that. Maybe...*

She straightened. "Do you guys have a golf cart here, or one of those all-terrain Mules people use around the barn?"

The dark-haired woman held out a hand. "I'm Reagan, Dr. Matthews—or Dr. Covington, I guess—Eli's wife. We sort of met at the rodeo and we've been exchanging emails over the past couple of weeks. Yes, we have half a dozen golf carts for guest use and four Mules for the cowboys to haul feed, tack and such. Why?"

Before Kenzie could answer, the other woman stepped in and took one of Kenzie's rough hands in both of her smooth, slender ones. "I'm Emmaline, Emma for short, and the last name's about to be Covington."

Kenzie squeezed Emma's hand in recognition. "You were the woman with Cade in Fort Worth."

"Yes." Emma blushed prettily.

Reagan shifted her attention to Kenzie. "The 2014 Kawasaki Mule with the four-inch lift kit and all-terrain tires has the best ride. Will that work?" she asked as she dug a key ring out of her pocket and began sifting through them. Finding the right one, she pulled it off and handed it over.

"Just like that?" Kenzie asked, surprised.

"I assume it has to do with getting Ty out of the house."

Kenzie nodded at the doctor. "It does."

Emma glanced at the house before meeting Kenzie's

curious stare. "He's changed, and we don't have a clue what to do for him. If you have a plan, I'm all for it."

"Can he walk at all?" Kenzie asked as she slipped the key into her jeans pocket and cracked her knuckles.

"A little. He's anxious, but he can do it. Just doesn't like us to watch him practice." Reagan considered Kenzie, seeming to weigh her next words. "He doesn't ever leave the house."

"I'm sure he's worried about how he'll be treated by the ranch hands. He's worked with them a long time?" Kenzie asked.

"Yeah." Reagan watched as one of those very hands rode a horse in close to the barn at a lazy trot, calling out a welcome to someone mending fence. "He's known them for years. Why?"

"He won't want them to think less of him." She shrugged under the weight of the women's curious stares. "It's pretty normal, really." Kenzie flushed when Reagan shot a quick glance at Emma, the look on her face asking how a rodeo-circuit cowgirl would know what was "normal" for a person recovering from an injury. She fought not to hunch her shoulders. "I majored in psychology. Graduated magna cum laude."

Reagan's entire assessment changed, her stance relaxing and her shoulders dropping some. "Very good to know. And everything you said is true. We've been coddling him a little too much."

Kenzie watched the goings-on around them for a minute before pulling the key out of her pocket and returning it to Reagan. "He'll feel safest with his brothers. Have them bring him down tomorrow after breakfast. If he protests, pick up his damn chair and carry him to the barn. Just make sure the area's clear." She closed her eyes for a brief moment and listened to Gizmo's second bugle. "I'm going to do what I can to ensure the horse is up for the visit."

She dug her truck keys out of her pocket.

"Where are you going?" Reagan asked, clearly confused.

"I need to get my own mare home and make plans to be back tomorrow for Gizmo's first physical therapy session."

Reagan shook her head, reaching behind her to begin braiding her hair into a French braid as she spoke. "It'll be easier if you just stay."

*No. Oh, no. I'm* not *getting roped into being the one to deal with the injured cowboy because these folks aren't willing to. No, no, no.*

But when Kenzie started into the—first—hundred reasons that came to mind as to why she couldn't... shouldn't...*wouldn't* stay, Emma stepped in. "Truly. There's a one-bedroom cabin vacant. It's nearest the barn and set up as a honeymoon suite. No one's renting it at the moment, so you're free to use the space. And your mare can stay here. I'm sure the barn will be okay for her." At Reagan's wheezed laughter, Emma's gaze snapped between them. "What? What did I say?"

The slightly shorter woman shook her head, swinging the tail of her braid. "The Malone barn is nicer than our house, Emma. Nicer, even, than the house you and Cade are building."

"I don't know about that," Kenzie objected, but once again, her input was overrun with the doctor's practical assessment.

"Look, Ms. Malone—"

She held up a hand. "Kenzie, please."

"Kenzie, then. It's no secret you're the sole heir to the Malone fortune. That's all well and good. That money has undoubtedly afforded you a different life than most have led, particularly here. 'Different' doesn't equal better or worse. Just...well, *different*."

"You're The Malone's daughter?" Emma's clear capitalization of her father's name made Kenzie want to smile, but she refrained. Barely.

Instead, she gave a single nod. "I'm sure you and I have our differences, but I know the value of hard work. My dad has money, yes. That didn't excuse me as a kid from chores any more than it exempted me from having to make my way through the dips, dives, turns and resentments of the male-dominated sport of cutting." She sighed and scrubbed her hands over her face. She was so tired, and at this point just wanted to lie down.

Emma fidgeted, twisting her fingers together until she formed a fist. She paused and seemed to struggle with whether or not to speak her mind. Finally she blurted out, "Are you the one who paid Ty's hospital bills?"

Kenzie didn't answer. She refused to admit she'd helped the man who'd been so wretched to her only moments ago. And she was sure that she, and her motives, had been the topic of many a Covington discussion.

She wound her hair up and then absently tucked it under her ball cap, trying to buy time.

The two women opposite her shared a look, and then Emma stepped forward and hugged her. "For all you've done for us, for all you've done without any reason other than it was the compassionate thing to do, stay. Please. Give us a chance to at least repay your kindness with some of our own."

Guilt wrapped around Kenzie's spine like a ribbon around a maypole.

Multilayered.

Fast.

Bright.

Tight.

Yet what these women shared, this tight family bond, was everything Kenzie had missed in her own family since Michael died, everything she craved. They were offering her a place inside that inner circle. It was too good to turn down. Impossible to refuse. Under the guise of the partnership, she could rediscover what it meant to have whole family unit, not a broken interpretation of what might have been. She could have this place, this space, this sense of belonging, even for the short time left until she handed Gizmo's recovery wholly to Reagan. It was selfish, but she wanted to experience what it felt like to be part of something outside the Malone name, something that had been built on hard work, sweat, tears and genuine talent versus parental expectation, unavoidable responsibility to grieving parents and the burden of obligation based on nothing more than her last name and bank balance.

This could blow up in her face on an epic scale. Ty could accuse her of lying and she'd have nothing with which to refute his allegations other than her own assertion she'd only done what he asked her to. Except the whole partnership thing. That was a big ol' lie. Nothing more, and nothing less. She should say no. She should get out of there before the brothers became involved and a similar obligation led them to open their homes, and their lives, to her.

Gizmo bugled again. The horse's third call echoed

across the open air, forlorn and lonely, a spirit lost between what had been and what now was.

That did it.

"Okay. I'll stay."

# 7

CADE AND ELI had insisted Ty get some sunshine this morning. Unfortunately, his brother's driving skills in the Mule had gone from pretty damn bad to downright crappy. Eli didn't seem *capable* of missing the rocks and staying out of the ruts as they traveled through the heart of the ranch. They were all fighting to keep from grunting and groaning as they crept along, every movement exaggerated thanks to the pace Eli insisted they keep. Ty would be lucky if he didn't refracture his neck or end up knocking a kidney free and having it land in the heel of his boot.

"Almost there," Cade called to him.

"Forced cheerfulness doesn't suit you," Ty snarked.

"No?" Cade asked with even more false enthusiasm. "Then, you know how I feel after living with your cranky ass the past couple of weeks. Being a total jerk hasn't suited you...or those of us who have to put *up* with you."

"Cut it out, both of you." Eli's reprimand was as effective as dry tinder tossed into a burgeoning wildfire.

"I don't understand why you insisted I come out this

morning." Ty, facing backward and with Cade at his side to help stabilize him, was beginning to sweat with the effort to stay upright. "This is stupid. I should be resting."

"All you do is 'rest,'" Cade answered with air quotes. "You're not putting much effort into your physical therapy, you're not doing the exercises in between sessions, and frankly, you're approaching the point where I'm going to take you for a walk one of us doesn't come back from. Hint? I'll make it home just fine."

Ty's temper shot north. "I broke my damn neck, Cade. What would you have me do? Jump right into the middle of the life I led? Maybe take a local girl out for a night of dancing and a little fun? Or better yet, why don't I get in the saddle and see how *that* goes?"

"Chickenshit," said Eli from the front seat.

Ty's jaw fell open as far as the brace would allow it.

Cade caught the look on his face and laid a hand on his shoulder before speaking to their eldest brother. "That might be taking it a little far."

"No, it isn't. If he's going to treat his body as if it's this fragile palm frond, getting up each day and refusing to push himself to grow and get stronger, then I'll call it like I see it. *Chickenshit.*" The Mule coasted to a stop, and the putter of the engine died when Eli pulled the key. "The truth sucks, particularly when you—*either* of you—don't want to hear it."

"Did you hear a word I said?" Ty demanded, forcing himself to slip from the rear-facing seat and, with the aid of his walker, get his feet under him before slowly rounding on Eli. His next words died on his lips, though, when he realized where they'd brought him.

*The barn.*

And that meant…

*Gizmo.*

"No." Voice hoarse, eyes gritty, Ty stumbled, but Eli and Cade each grabbed an arm to steady him. "I can't do this. Take me to the house. Now."

"You want to go back?" Eli let him go and slipped into the driver's seat, cranked the engine over and took off at breakneck speed. "Walk," he shouted as he sped away.

"I can't…" He shuffled his feet around until he faced Cade. "I can't do this."

"Huge difference between *can't* and *won't*." His older brother settled the walker in front of Ty and moved out of reach. He pulled out an apple from his pocket and tossed it to Ty. "Time to stop lying to yourself. You may not *want* to do this, but you can. Suck it up and get it over with. Tell Gizmo I said hello. I'll be within shouting range if you run into trouble." Then Cade spun on his heel and walked away, rounding the corner of the barn and disappearing from sight.

Movement in the barn told Ty he wasn't alone. That he couldn't see who it was irritated him. He didn't want this. Didn't want to be stared at as if he was some crash-test dummy. Didn't want to be the topic of conversation in the bunkhouse. Didn't want to be the subject of discussion. Didn't want anyone's pity. He could withstand—had withstood—a lot, but not that. Never that.

Cade's accusation that Ty had thrown in the towel stung. He'd tried so hard to retain some sense of himself, that same sense of humor, the same wit and flirty banter with the opposite sex. It didn't come easy. Not when his life had been reduced to a series of moments, a few breaths that refused to come and a heart that stopped beating. And yeah, it had happened that way. It was the one thing he remembered in an otherwise void of blackness.

He remembered he'd been looking at Kenzie when his heart stopped. She'd watched him fight for every breath he could steal, witnessed his heart stall out, and she'd stood there and cried as darkness took him under. She'd wept for him, but not once had she reached out to him.

*Sure as hell kept her hands all over my horse*, he silently muttered.

Shifting his walker to face the gaping maw of the barn door, he took his first step toward the dim interior. Paused. A second step. Another pause. His breath came hard and shallow. His head felt extremely heavy on his fragile neck. Walking took more concentration, more sheer effort, than it ever had. Sweat dotted his nape. He wanted to return to the comfort of his wheelchair. His heart, that defiant organ, thundered in his chest, and he waited, sure in the knowledge that it could quit again without warning. Every sensation was horrible in its own right. Combined? He was overwhelmed with the urge to tear the barn down with his bare hands, one board at a time, in lieu of being emotionally deconstructed in the same fashion.

"I can't." Wiping his brow, he glanced around. "I can't do this."

He struggled to keep his balance as he attempted to maneuver the walker toward the house. Lord help him, he was as weak as a newborn foal. His legs refused to stabilize. He had to get out of here, though, and he'd do it on his own. Pride would keep him upright far longer than stamina ever would. And when he ran out of pride? When he couldn't go any farther without help? He'd call his brothers. They could pick him up and drive him to the house. This was, after all, their fault. He never would have come down to the barn of his own free will. This was a mistake—an *epic* mistake.

Then Gizmo called out, the sound heart wrenching.

Chest tightening impossibly, he took finite steps until he was pointed toward the barn again. Moving slowly, fear bore down on him with every step. By the time he crossed the threshold into the barn, his defenses had been thoroughly stripped away, his emotions raw and exposed.

For better or worse, he stood where it had all started— where he'd found a way to live, to be more than the youngest Covington, more than a playboy screwup, more than he'd ever thought he'd be with more than he'd ever thought he might have.

He'd had everything he'd wanted.

Then that bitch Life had found a way to take it all away from him.

KENZIE HAD HEARD the Mule stop, then charge away. Voices had risen in confrontation before Cade had announced he was leaving Ty to fend for himself. She was confident the middle Covington brother hovered nearby, though. He wouldn't leave his younger brother alone to fend for himself. She knew Cade well enough to be sure he was far too loyal for that.

Then she heard the shuffle-step, shuffle-step of Ty's progress. She wanted to go to him, to help, but he had to do this for himself. Her job was to stay out of the way. She'd only observe. If an issue arose that put either Ty or Gizmo at risk, she'd text one of the brothers. Or, heaven forbid, both.

She was glad she'd changed her mind about Ty visiting Gizmo. Both animal and man would heal faster if they had each other to lean on. A bond like these two had was as rare as it was beautiful.

When Ty neared the barn, Kenzie slipped into the deep shadows between the haystack and the tack room to best watch the man move. The determination on his face had been tempered by a bevy of other emotions, all of which were horrible to witness. His stop-and-start gait left his footing unsure, and he leaned on his walker so heavily the wheels sank first into the soft dirt and then, when he reached the barn, the mulched alleyway bisecting the stalls.

He stopped inside the giant doorway and closed his eyes, and she thought he might have given up. Half of her wanted to rail at him for quitting while the other half wanted to go to him, wrap him in her arms and offer to help carry the burden. In an abstract way, they'd been that person to each other over the past few years. This, however, was different. *Decidedly* different. This wasn't about mutual gratification or losing a couple of hours to pleasure to get one's mind off something. Rather, it was about choosing to embrace life instead of letting circumstance steal it from a loosened grasp.

She stayed where she was.

Ty finally opened his eyes and focused his gaze on Gizmo's stall.

Kenzie originally wanted to put the horse in the stall at the far end of the barn, where it would be easier to access the swimming pool she was having installed. It dawned on her she hadn't mentioned the pool to anyone here. Oops. She'd get on that as soon as this moment with Ty and Gizmo passed. Right now, though, the man and his horse were the priority. The family had entrusted her to see to Gizmo's well-being while they were focused on Ty.

*They trust me.*

The knowledge stole her breath. Fist pressed to her abdomen, she forced herself to breathe slowly. That was when it happened.

A gelding in stall five, halfway down the stable alley-way on the north side, stuck his head over his stall door and spotted Ty. The horse went nuts. Pawing the door, he tossed his head and snorted, rolled his eyes and stretched his lips out, flapping them like sheets in the wind.

Ty saw the animal and froze. "Gilligan," he croaked, the sound raw, the painful reality undiluted. "I'll get to you in a minute, my man."

More horses appeared, peering out of their stalls to see what the hullabaloo was about. Recognizing Ty, they neighed and stomped their feet and gave every sound of joy one might expect from an excited herd of horses.

Kenzie grinned and then glanced at Ty to gauge his reaction. What she found wiped the smile off her face.

Ty stood staring at Gizmo's stall, eyes wide as tea saucers and face as pale as cream. He shook. Not mild shaking, but the kind that was closer to a seizure. He stared straight ahead, his gaze narrowed on the stall door in front of him where no head had emerged.

Then, Gizmo was there. He moved with a faltering gait, his head bobbing in counterbalance to his limp, but it didn't change the fact that his head appeared over the stall door.

Ty physically sagged so much he nearly fell. Shoulders shaking, she watched as the man she'd always known as strong, indefatigable and hardheaded fell apart. He moved forward through sheer force of will.

Tears spilled down the cheek he unknowingly presented in profile to her. His lips moved in what she would guess could only be an invocation, and Gizmo's ears strained toward the man as if he listened to every word.

Ty finally made it to the horse and stopped.

With incredible tenderness, Gizmo lowered his head and pressed his broad face into Ty's chest. The animal loosed an audible sigh that said more than the most powerful words ever would.

Moving with infinite care, Ty rested one hand on the side of Gizmo's cheek and bowed his head. Tears fell faster. "What the hell were you thinking, you giant lunk? Nothing—no prize, no winnings, no title—*nothing* is worth what you put us through. If you thought different, you're an idiot." The last was offered with such soft condemnation that it was impossible to know whether Ty was referring to himself or his horse.

Gizmo didn't move, just leaned into Ty and held perfectly still as Ty ran his hands over every inch of hide he could reach. The horse's long-lashed eyes slowly closed as he relaxed further. His bottom lip wobbled, and Ty smiled, the reaction softening the grief that had etched itself onto his face.

Never had Kenzie witnessed such a private reunion, and she hated herself more than a little for hiding in the shadows and watching such an intimate moment.

The other horses calmed down as Ty continued to talk, their faces turned toward him, ears perked and eyes alert.

It was only their silence that allowed Kenzie to hear his next statement.

"You and I both know that if it wasn't for Kenzie, you wouldn't be here right now. It changes things between us, me and her. Before? It was fun. I think it might have even been headed somewhere. I don't know. But now? I owe her a debt I can never repay. I *owe* her. And we can't ever go back to what we had before. Hell, *none* of us can go back to what we had before. At least you lived—" Ty's voice broke, and he fought to regain control. "She saved you when I couldn't." He let go of the walker and placed his other hand on Gizmo's chin, lifting his head so they were face to face. "Her money did for you what I couldn't—got you the best of everything. I wouldn't ever have been able to afford the Galbreath Center. She's done right by us, so I have to set my pride aside and find a way to thank her." He closed his eyes. "I wish I could reset the clock on this whole thing, but there's no such thing as a do-over. Not for you. Not for me. Not for her. And definitely not for me *and* her."

The floor fell out from under Kenzie. He thought there could have been more between them? That maybe, just maybe, they could have been something?

The words changed everything. And nothing. He resented the financial debt that he'd incurred, and she resented that money could create issues where none need exist. But she understood why he saw it as something he could never set right between them. It was debt she'd accrued based on a single promise—a promise she'd made when she'd thought she might lose Ty. The raw feelings she had for him meant she'd given her word without thinking, and she'd followed through on her promise because that was just who she was.

It would have been so much simpler if she hadn't fallen for him, if she'd remained detached instead of letting the walls between them crumble, the same walls she'd worked so hard to create when they'd first met. But she hadn't. She'd opened the door to him and begun to fall for the one man from whom she'd sworn she'd never expect more than fun and respect.

Hidden in the shadows, she watched Ty with Gizmo. Her heart ached as if it had been pierced. She swallowed the sound of distress that choked her. There had to be a way out, a way that everyone could get what they wanted, what they *needed*, and no one had to get hurt.

There just had to be.

# 8

TY FOUGHT TO control his emotions. If he got stressed out, Gizmo would pick up on it. But seeing his horse like this, stiff and hurting, divided him. One half wanted to rage against the injustices heaped upon each of them, him and Gizmo. The other half wanted to fold into himself and crumple to the floor until someone came along and picked up the pieces. He'd never been a man to give up when hardship reared its head. But this was more than your average hardship. This particular experience was better described as having been TKO'ed by Hardship and beaten up by his posse members, Pain, Misery and Hopelessness.

A small sound caught his attention, a noise a horse wouldn't make. He grabbed his walker and, legs trembling with exhaustion, faced the direction of the sound. Narrowing his eyes, he stared into the sliver of dense shadow between the end of the tack room and the tall base of the haystack. At first he saw nothing, but, as his eyes adjusted to the limited light, he realized someone was standing there.

"I know you're hiding back there. Come on out." His

tone was intentionally gentle but left no room for either discussion or dissention.

The shadowy figure shifted, stopped and then stepped into the light.

He'd expected a guest, someone who'd been caught in the barn when Eli and Cade had kicked him out of the Mule. What he got was his worst nightmare and deepest desire all rolled into one.

*Mackenzie Malone.*

"What the hell are you doing here?" he demanded, the soothing cadence of his earlier words lost to immediate temper.

"I was out here checking on Gizmo when you showed up. I tried to leave, but I couldn't get the door at the end of the alleyway to open. The latch stuck. It left me either confronting you or trying to wait you out. I chose the latter." She shoved her hair off her face on a huff. "How did you figure out I was here anyway?"

"You need to learn to keep quiet if you don't want to be discovered skulking about."

"I wasn't skulking."

"Fine. Let's call it what it is—sticking your nose where it doesn't belong." He snatched his walker up and did his best to make tracks for the barn door, hollering for Cade and Eli as he went. When his brothers failed to appear, Ty quietly cursed them. *Freaking brothers. They know she's out here.*

Working to keep his breathing level, he forced one foot in front of the other in as fast a retreat as he could muster. Even his best efforts couldn't stop his temper from spilling out of his mouth. "'Fess up. How are they getting you to do their dirty work, watching over me? You obviously don't need the money, and we clearly don't have it to spare, so that's not it. What did they promise you?"

"Can't I simply do something because it's right?"

He hated the way her voice seemed smaller, swallowed by the empty space above them. "You and I don't have that kind of relationship."

"We've never had anything that remotely *resembles* a relationship, Ty." Kenzie moved toward him, her hips swinging as they always did when she was walking off a good mad...or building up to one. "You always made it perfectly clear we were friends with benefits. Never anything more. I accepted that without comment and without fussing. So don't you go throwing attitude at me, acting as if I've somehow wronged you by doing *exactly* what you asked me to do. I used my own discretion in saving Gizmo's life. And my judgment calls kept him from being put down and guaranteed he'd recover. I gave him a chance at life. The least you could do is offer up, oh, I don't know, a thank-you. But you won't, will you? Or is it that you can't, Ty? Which one is true?" She closed in on him. "Both, I'd wager. Why? Because it's so clear that you're pissed at the world, angry about the hand that's been dealt you. It's inhibited your ability to do anything more than feel sorry for yourself."

She'd closed the distance between them and was leaning into his face as she threw out that last word. Fury raced through his veins, chased by guilt at the way he'd lashed out at her and the knowledge she was right. The hell he'd admit it, though.

She smirked, her eyes never leaving his as she goaded him further. "Surely the ever-argumentative Tyson Covington has *something* to say."

Ty didn't think, didn't consider the consequences.

He just gripped the back of her neck and pulled her into him. Their mouths came together without apology, without compromise, without softness. This, this primal thing that always hung between them, proved bigger than words and defied any tenderness his wounded heart might crave. He needed passion, needed to know he had survived, needed to feel something—*anything*— other than the ever-present pain.

He owned the kiss, sure of himself in this one thing. She responded to his wordless directions, sighed into his mouth and gave herself over to the driving force of his desire. Still, she didn't let him dominate her but made him work for it, made him chase the particular tilt of her chin, the touch and retreat of her tongue, the nibble of her teeth on his lips.

Her chest brushed against his.

Ty didn't think too much about keeping his balance. He simply held on and let her come to him, encouraging her to take what she wanted and give him what he needed in exchange. Somehow, though, his need seemed larger, more visceral, than simple desire. Of course, given the way his body responded, his cock hardening in a painful rush and his heart thundering so loudly in his ears that he struggled to hear anything else, he wasn't going to dismiss the power of desire.

Kenzie moved again in an effort to better accommodate the limited motion his neck brace allowed. Despite the clothing between them, he could feel her nipples harden against his chest. Then she sighed his name. It was her response that grounded Ty in the moment, gave him his footing and offered him the kind of reassurance he'd been searching for since he'd woken from the coma. Here, with her, he found safety, a surety of self, a sense of purpose. He could give her what she desired. And what she desired was him.

Yet the experience of holding her in his arms wasn't all that simple. True, he wanted nothing more than to lose himself in her, to take the warmth she offered and let her spend the morning convincing him that he was, indeed, alive. He also wanted to rail against her for things that weren't her fault—the fact that she had two good legs, strong arms, a steady gait and, above all, the freedom to do as she pleased.

Conflicted, he pulled away, ending the kiss.

Her eyelids fluttered open and she blinked, her pupils wide enough they almost consumed the cornflower blue of her irises. "It's hard to fight with you when you kiss me senseless."

One corner of his mouth kicked up despite the fact that he tried his best to not smile. "That's the point."

"Yeah, well, it's cheating." She smiled, contentment radiating from her in waves.

The realization she was happy nearly knocked the wind out of him. *How can she stand here and be happy?*

Fighting to regain control of the moment, he glanced over her shoulder at Gizmo, who stood with his head up, ears forward and eyes bright. Ty shook his head and then forced himself to meet Kenzie's gaze. "It's not cheating. I've just never been one to depend on words when actions get the job done without complicating things."

And with her, it always worked that way. Words hadn't ever been necessary between them. In fact, words tended only to muddle things. Without words, what existed between them was, and had always been, a simple case of mutual want that ruled the moment and drove their actions.

She closed her eyes and breathed deeply. "No sense complicating anything."

"You know I don't do complicated, darlin'."

She stiffened, her fingers digging into his arms. The smile that had pulled at the corners of her mouth disappeared, her expressive face closing down.

Ty wanted to retrieve the words, take them back. He wanted to figure out how to say what had to be said— that he wasn't available for more than the moment, never again, not even for her—without stealing that blissful look from her face. But his old man had taught him early on that words, once offered up, could never be taken back.

KENZIE TRIED NOT to react. Honest.

She failed.

And she didn't fail on a minor level. This failure proved epic. And the longer Ty's words looped through her mind, the more her reaction gained first traction, then speed and finally purpose.

She'd heard him admit to Gizmo that there might have been something between them. Then to her face he'd crushed that hope.

She knew her eyes had shuttered, knew her face wore a neutral expression. It was a tactic her father had mastered for negotiating, as well as in difficult social situations. Her dad used the opportunity to craft a strategic response. Kenzie had spent a lifetime emulating the very same affect but had never expected it to come in so handy. She was surprised to realize that, for her, strategy wasn't a factor. She needed the time to figure out how she was going to hide the body, because killing Tyson Covington had taken on spectacular appeal.

Stepping away from the man lest she strangle him, she gave a curt nod. "Sure thing, *darlin'*. Why complicate somethin' so simple as a friends-with-bennies arrangement, right?" Her tone was so caustic it should have burned the barn down around them.

"Kenzie, I—"

"No need to finish that sentence," she volunteered. "Mixing up something as straightforward as this is foolish. I get it. You made sure of that."

He tried to smile at her, but whatever he saw in her face made that smile falter. "I should go."

"Typical." The single word cracked across the air like a rifle's report. "Things get uncomfortable and you find the nearest exit." She crossed her arms under her breasts. "Go on, then. Call one of your brothers. They'll be the fastest way out of here for you. Eli!" she shouted. "Cade! Bring the Mule, would you? This cowboy wants to ride into the sunset." She rounded on Ty, chest heaving. "I'm sure they'll be here in no time, rushing in to save their little brother from assuming responsibility. And since you won't—assume responsibility, that is—I will. I'll manage Gizmo and his recovery."

Ty's eyes blazed with undisguised anger. "Excuse me?"

"I said—"

"I heard what you said," he snapped. "It isn't a matter of me *choosing* not to manage Gizmo's recovery, and you know it."

"No, Ty. What I 'know' is that you're supposed to be recovering from an injury. Instead, you're acting as if you're sitting around waiting to die. What I 'know' is that if you don't get your ass down here and invest in your animals, someone's going to do it for you. I can't speak to your other horses, but as far as Gizmo is concerned, that someone will be me." Realization almost blinded her. This was her chance to solidify the lies and make them truths. "If I have to take over, I'll do it based on the extreme investments—both financial and personal—that *you* requested I make to ensure Gizmo's well-being. That was the foundation of this partnership after all."

"Like hell!" His shout reverberated through the barn. "I want the partnership dissolved."

"Yeah? How, *exactly*, do you suggest we accomplish that? Are you going to repay me for doing exactly what you asked me to do, Ty? For being financially responsible for all of the medical bills and seeing the horse through recovery? Or maybe you think if you walk away, it will just *go* away. Is that it? Do you honestly believe I should have done it—*any* of it—without expecting fair recompense? After all, you said it yourself just moments ago. We don't have the kind of relationship that would warrant me doing something out of the sheer goodness of my heart."

"What heart?" he spat.

"Obviously the one Daddy bought me as my sweet-sixteen present. It was black, to match my truck." Her stomach pitched and rolled like a dinghy on a violent sea. She'd never lorded money over anyone. Ever. But she couldn't turn back now without losing the ground she'd gained. This had become as much an issue of defending her pride as covering her lies.

When she'd been in college and struggled with a senior-level business class, her dad had sat her down and explained that negotiations were much like poker. There was a little shuffling, a lot of bluffing and even

more posturing. If you sat at a table where you were unsure about the other players, the most important thing
to do was salvage the hand you were dealt. That meant
playing it smart, hard and close to the chest. It made your
opponent wonder what you held, and it bought you time
to convince him that, even with a total crap hand, you
were bound to win. The point, he'd said, was to hold
until you were forced to fold.

Kenzie stared up at Ty and narrowed her eyes as he
did the same.

She. Wasn't. Folding. Not on this. Not ever.

She took a large step backward and crossed her arms.
"You don't get to choose in this, Ty. Not when you left
me with both personal and financial responsibility for
Gizmo's care. You left me alone!" she shouted. "You left
me to decide whether to euthanize that magnificent animal and put him out of his misery, or walk the road to
recovery with him *because you wouldn't.*" She looked
at Gizmo's stunning gray-and-black coloring, those ice-
blue eyes watching her with a shrewd awareness that
always unnerved her a bit. "You want to settle this?"
she asked so quietly Ty instinctively leaned toward her.

"You know I do," he said through gritted teeth.

She faced Ty then and let the hammer fall. "I'll accept
short-term breeding rights to Gizmo as full satisfaction
of all monies owed."

"Like. Hell," he said again. He pulled his cowboy hat
off and tunneled his fingers through his hair. "He's off-
limits, Malone."

"I've invested more than twenty thousand dollars in
your medical bills. I've also sunk more than eighty thousand dollars in your horse's bills. Where he's concerned,
I'll see another twenty-three thousand dollars in the pool

installation and ten thousand dollars in miscellaneous physical therapy costs."

All color drained from Ty's face. "I didn't realize…" His Adam's apple bobbed. "I'll repay you. With interest. We'll set something up. Just leave Gizmo alone." He swallowed hard enough for her to hear it, and then he dropped his own hammer. "Please."

She ground her teeth together, ashamed of herself and furious with him for pushing her into this. *Save Gizmo*, he'd pleaded with her after she'd thought she'd lost him, the man she'd begun to care for despite her best efforts to remain detached. She'd gone further than he'd likely ever expected her to go, and despite it all, he wouldn't give her an inch in return. He still considered her genetics so inferior to his that he refused to allow Gizmo to be part of her breeding program.

She sucked in a sharp breath, the dry, icy air burning her lungs even as it froze them. No. He couldn't use her like this. She wouldn't be some bottomless ATM that spewed cash on demand and never had a single deposit in return. If she didn't set this boundary, she'd never be more than this to him. She opened her mouth to say just that, but Eli pulled up in the Mule.

Ty began his shuffling turn toward the barn door and his best—only—means of escape.

"Everything okay?" Eli called, all good cheer and hopefulness.

"As okay as it can be when you have a rabid fox in the henhouse and find your shotgun's out of ammo," Ty answered.

Eli shot Kenzie a glance. When she didn't respond, his eyes narrowed. "What happened?"

"Nothing." She managed to issue the single word

without her voice wavering. Chest tight, she forced herself to continue. "Your brother wasn't aware I'd expect repayment for both his and his horse's medical bills."

Eli's eyes tightened at the corners before he offered a shallow nod. "We'll manage as a family."

"No, we won't." Ty stumbled, but he righted himself before either she or Eli could grab him. "I'll work it out. I have a few horses I can sell."

Kenzie's heart constricted as Eli erupted in a veritable tirade. She knew it would kill Ty to sell part of his breeding stock. Yes, he'd retain the heart—Gizmo—but the body would be weakened. Could she be responsible for that?

That wasn't the part that ate at her, though. She'd never acted the part of a spoiled diva, not like this, and she was beyond mortified.

Eli helped Ty into the backseat of the Mule and Cade appeared as if summoned, sat next to his younger brother and shot Kenzie a glare that, in theory, should have turned her to stone. He'd obviously heard enough of the exchange with Ty to draw his own conclusions.

*Freaking fabulous.*

The brothers pulled away, Ty's entire focus on Gizmo. The man she'd given up her dream of nationals for never once looked at her as the Mule rounded the bend and headed for the main house.

Kenzie retrieved her cell and called home.

# 9

JACK MALONE ANSWERED on the third ring. "Hey, baby. What's new? Everything going okay at the Covington place?"

"I need to talk to you about that, Dad," she replied softly as she moved toward Gizmo's stall. The stud horse watched her, anxious for the treats she carried. He nosed her pockets, lipping loose fabric eagerly and huffing at her. Determined not to add his disappointment in her to everyone else's running tally, she pulled out a couple worse-for-wear sugar cubes and, pinning the cell phone between her ear and shoulder, offered the sweets to the horse one at a time.

"You're there, aren't you?" The elder Malone's voice had a faint echo thanks to crappy cell service. That connection didn't disguise his concern, though.

She sighed. "Does it make a difference?"

"Of course it matters, honey. I want to know where you are. That way, if you need me, I can ride in on my white horse. A man can't just charge blindly, you understand." When she didn't respond to his teasing, he sobered. "You came by, loaded Indie up and then left without speaking to me. I haven't seen you in two months." He paused, his breath rasping across the microphone. When he finally broke the silence, his tone came across far softer than before. "Are you okay? Has something happened? You can talk to me, Mackenzie. Always. About anything."

Her shoulders hunched. The implied censure, delivered with parental effectiveness despite the fact that she was twenty-four years old, worked. "You weren't home when I picked Indie up. That's all it was."

"You could have waited," he countered. "Any one of the hands would have told you I'd be home before sundown."

"Sorry." She hated having apologies wrung out of her, particularly because she never could do the same in reverse. Moving away from the apology altogether seemed prudent. "I had to be at the Covington place to arrive with Ty's stud." She reached out and tickled the lips of the horse under discussion.

"I understand." Her father took a deep breath. "How is Gizmo?"

"Fair." She heard a tractor fire up on his end. Kenzie imagined the way the belch of diesel exhaust would sully the cool Colorado air of the Malone place, could see the way the fields sloped away from the mountains, could almost feel the rumble of the big engine through her torso. "You feeding this early in the season? I thought the grass looked pretty good."

"I want to increase the protein intake of the yearlings in pasture one, so I'm pulling a few round bales to run down to them. Have some good blood on the ground, thanks to you."

His pride in her, so evident in both word and tone,

made her squirm. That she'd lied to him and, worse, let that lie run on, gain a life of its own and encourage him to develop expectations of her she'd never be able to live up to? She had to shut it down. "Dad, I…" She stalled out.

"What's wrong, honey? Talk to me."

*He loves me more than I deserve.* This was the man she'd loved all her life. This was the man she related to with such ease. This was the man she'd always sought advice from over the years, particularly after losing Michael. And in return, he'd begun to talk to her about the ranch the way he once had talked to Michael. He'd learned to trust her instincts and valued her input because she never pulled her punches, never simply said what he wanted to hear because he was Jack Malone. Not until now anyway. That particular realization doubled the weight of her guilt. She had to admit she'd lied. He wouldn't stop loving her, wouldn't turn her away, wouldn't shut her out. Not as Ty had.

But when she opened her mouth, it wasn't the truth that came out. Instead, she found herself recounting everything that had just happened, from the family's insistence that she stay on the ranch to listening to Ty's private monologue with his horse to the harsh words more recently exchanged. The only thing she omitted was the kiss. When the last of her troubles passed her lips, the only response she got was one of absolute silence. Nausea rushed up her throat so rapidly she fought not to choke on it. "Dad?"

"He's reneging on the partnership?" The hostility in the question was hardly banked.

"What? No! Not exactly," she said. "He doesn't remember—" *Because there's nothing* to *remember*, her subconscious interjected. *Go on. Tell him. Tell him that you not only lied, you kept the dishonesty running for months between the two of you. You've had ample opportunities to come clean. Tell him you didn't because... Why? Why haven't you?* She couldn't explain it to him because she didn't have a remotely plausible answer for herself.

"What is it, then?" Jack Malone pressed. "Because I know what you've spent."

"Are you checking up on me?" The idea appalled her.

"Not checking up so much as ensuring you had everything you needed while you were in Ohio."

"Sell it to someone else, Dad. You know my initial trust fund deposit was enough to live off for the rest of my life. You don't have to watch over me."

Jack Malone hardly paused, let alone yielded his position. "I've seen the checks you've written, Mackenzie. That man has sure as hell taken your money without batting an eye. I will *not* have him take advantage of your kindheartedness."

She stepped away from Gizmo, her hands trembling so hard she feared she'd drop the phone. Pinning it between her ear and shoulder, she shoved her hands into her pockets and fought for calm. If her dad believed Ty had taken advantage of her, there would be hell to pay. She had to stop the momentum she could feel him gaining as his parental instincts kicked in. "Dad, it's not what you think."

"Then, what is it, Mackenzie? Spell it out for me, because from where I sit? It looks very much as if he's abused your generosity. You can't let people spin some bullshit story just to get what they want from you, particularly when you're dealing with this kind of money and no return."

"I thought you were fine with it." The words were strained, the air in her lungs slowly pushing out as an invisible band of panic six inches wide torqued down on her ribs, increasing in pressure until black dots danced through her vision.

She had to slow down, regain control of the moment, her emotions, her situation. Now. Before it got worse. Panic attacks had been daily events after her brother died until intensive counseling and medication had taught her how to control them. Then they'd stopped. She hadn't had an attack in years. This one had struck so fast she hadn't been able to talk herself down.

"Dad," she whispered, panic winding its way through that single word.

"Mackenzie?" Jack's tone changed in an instant. "Talk to me, baby girl. I can hear you breathing hard. What happened? What upset you? Was it me? I'm so sorry, Kenzie. Just slow down, we don't have to deal with this right now." The sound of ice clinking against glass preceded the *glug* of liquid splashing into the same. He swallowed hard, then his voice was back, smoother, calmer. "Slow down, Mackenzie. Just slow down." He took another sip, smaller this time. "This isn't easy for either of us."

"What?" she wheezed. *Awfully early for him to hit the bottle.* "What do you mean?"

"The panic. It's chock-full of the worst moments of our lives. You relive it, I relive it." He sighed, the sound weighted. "You were too young to lose your brother, let alone see it happen." The sound of another sip. "It tore us all up."

"I know." Forcing herself to draw slow, deep breaths, Kenzie refocused on Gizmo. "It won't hurt me to practice a random act of kindness, Dad."

"Financially? No, it won't, though I'm a bit irritated you're wasting Malone money on a man trying to back out on his promise. A person's only as good as his word, and you know I'm right. But that isn't the only position to consider. There are the emotional costs you're incurring." He waited. When she didn't respond, he continued, his voice rougher, harder, less compassionate that she'd ever heard it. "I won't have your heart broken by some two-bit country kid who thinks he can bat his eyes at you, promise you a partnership and get you to fork over the cash to see him through a hard spot."

"You did *not* just imply I'm too…too…*female* to be able to hold my own with a 'two-bit country kid,'" she said on a raw whisper.

"If Michael were here, I'd have him over there right now to see that the Covington kid kept his word. Your brother would have done it, too."

"Dad—" she started, paused, then started again. "Dad, I'd like to think Michael would have trusted me to handle this on my own. And I'd like to think you would do the same." The irony wasn't lost on her. She was asking for his trust when she was giving nothing trustworthy in return. She'd never hated herself quite so much as she did right then.

"Your mother and I are concerned about you, honey. You're living a very lonely life right now, chasing that national title like it's the be-all and end-all. Now you've created this partnership that could make your line into something, and you're less interested in it than you are in the man who's trying to screw you out of your fair share."

"If you only knew," she muttered.

After an interminable silence, a silence in which Kenzie felt the pressures of his expectations building in her chest, he spoke. "Losing Michael wrecked this family." The words were offered like a reverent eulogy, not a decade-old memory, and it stung.

"I'm well aware of that. I lived through it," she said in a tight voice. *It* and *the aftermath.*

"Don't get smart with me." Jack Malone paused, seemingly searching for the right words. "Michael's loss left a hole in our lives, a hole we'll never fill again. Not because we don't want to, mind you, but because we can't. If that makes us a little overprotective of you as our only child, you'll just have to come to terms with it. You're all we've got left."

Her father continued, but Kenzie hardly heard the last of her dad's words before disconnecting the call. The conversation had stopped for her when he'd said she couldn't fill the hole that had been left by Michael. She'd spent a decade trying so hard to be both son and daughter to her parents, to be a strong enough person-ality to fill that emotional vacancy her brother had left. She'd failed on an epic level. Now, knowing her efforts to be both daughter and lost son to her parents had failed? Hearing him say it out loud? Fully aware she'd only be disappointing him further when she admitted her decep-tion? Well, she hadn't thought she'd be able to hate her-self any more. How miserably wrong she'd been.

TY COULDN'T GET the taste of Kenzie off his lips. He brushed his teeth. He drank a Coke. He considered smoking a cigar. That only reminded him of their last game of strip poker, the one where he'd been down to one sock and his boxers. She'd been tossing out cards while wearing nothing but a green dealer's visor, her bra and a black thong. A cigar had dangled from the corner of her mouth. Light had danced through her hair, and every time she'd moved, her smooth skin had pulled taut over that flat belly. Sure, it had been sexy. But it was nothing compared to the way her lips had wrapped around the butt of the cigar and kicked up at one corner when he'd lost the next hand in spectacular fashion. Oh, and his boxers. He'd lost those, too. She had immediately declared herself the winner and claimed him as her prize.

They hadn't slept that night.

"Damn it!" He slammed his closet door shut and collapsed into his wheelchair so hard he had to put a foot out to keep from tipping over. Settling, he wheeled over to the window in his temporary bedroom and looked up. "I'm seriously getting sick of this."

He shoved the window open a crack. A rush of crisp, snow-laden air washed over him and made the hair on his arms stand up at the chill. He needed the opportunity to cool off. Kenzie had left his blood so close to the boiling point that he couldn't think. Even now, all he wanted was to get his hands on her again and to have her put her hands on him. He just had to get her out of his system, then he'd see her off the ranch and out of his life. For good.

He heard the sound of a single horse's hooves pounding the earth. He stretched to peer out the window.

*Who is it? Windows are too tall. So either stand and see or sit and wonder, Covington.*

Curiosity won the internal debate as the sound grew

nearer, the tempo increasing as the horse picked up speed in order to charge up the hill.

*The rider's sticking to the road. Is something wrong? Has something happened? Could be one of the ranch hands on his way to fetch either Eli or Cade.*

He wanted the cowboy to be coming after *him*, coming to ask *him* for advice, ask *him* for help. It used to be that way. Not anymore. No one asked him for anything anymore.

Everyone from Kenzie to Eli had told him that was his own fault. Their theory? If he'd make an effort to re-engage not only with others but with life in general, folks wouldn't feel so awkward about approaching him. They'd start to seek him out again. He just had to make sure they knew they were welcome. But that was the problem. He wasn't at all sure they *were* welcome. He didn't want to be gawked at, didn't want to be—

Those pounding hooves drew closer still.

Screw it. He wasn't standing up. He was too tired and he hurt, no matter how little Kenzie thought of his excuse. *Excuse...*

"Damn if she's going to get me questioning myself," he groused. "Incoming!" he called into the house. Then he waited.

No answer.

"Hey!" he hollered. "I said there's a rider incoming!"

More silence.

Temper brewing, Ty grabbed the windowsill and pulled, hoisting himself up to peer out the wide but narrow bank of windows that ran nearly the full length of the wall. The breeze carried the smells of dust and crushed grass and animal through the window. Fresh and pungent, they tickled his nose and wordlessly encouraged him to draw in a deep breath. Then he choked when he recognized the rider, hunched over the animal's neck, riding hell-bent for leather up the main road as she headed deeper into the ranch.

*Kenzie.*

She didn't take in nearby scenery but kept her gaze focused far ahead. She didn't stop when a cowboy called out to her. Strangest of all, she didn't acknowledge a group of young kids, their trustworthy little ponies plodding along in single file as they carried their charges home from a trail ride.

Kenzie morphed into the Pied Piper around children. Little cowboys and cowgirls alike flocked to her at exhibitions and rodeos, clamoring to gain, and keep, her attention. She loved the littlest ones most, though she never admitted it.

So to see her fly by kids, her mare's jets set on wide open, without offering a greeting? No. That rang all kinds of bells, each of them chiming "wrong" in a different tone.

Ty watched her go, her shape growing ever smaller as the wind carried her dust trail off at a brisk clip. Never easing up, she and her mare crested the hill behind the house and disappeared. He sank into his chair, lost in thought. What kind of skeleton did a woman have in her closet that held that much sway over her? To chase her out into the elements in such a blind panic?

*Wasn't me, that's for sure. She had no problem holding her own with me out there. Frustrating woman, calling it as she sees it. To hell with everybody else's opinion. And changing her mind is as ridiculous as trying to take that goat from the T. rex in* Jurassic Park. *You know you'll never walk away with more than the blood-*

*ied scraps of your pride, and that's* after *you scrape the pieces together.*

"She's not right about me," he said to the empty room. Sitting deeper in his chair, he rubbed his aching belly. He should fix a sandwich or something to ease the mild nausea that had settled deep in his gut as he watched her thunder past the house. "She's not right," he repeated with more force.

That was when he stopped, stunned at the realization of what he'd just done.

He'd controlled his descent from the window to the wheelchair. And he'd done it without help or a single conscious thought. For the first time since the accident, he'd moved without stiff reserve and fearful awareness of every ache, pain... Hell, every threatening twinge.

With his mind tangled up with what had just happened, Ty absently moved toward the doorway, intent on wheeling himself to the kitchen...and came face-to-face with Reagan. Heat flamed across his cheeks at her stunned appearance. His chin came up a notch. "What?"

His sister-in-law looked at him, then his chair and then him again. She raised a hand and held it halfway to her mouth before letting it fall. Her eyes were wide. "You stood. On your own. With so little effort. How? When? And why didn't you tell anyone you could do this, Ty?" Skepticism vied with amazement in that green-eyed gaze. It unnerved him. Yet no amount of curiosity could dim the inherent compassion shining from her, a beacon of hope in the muted afternoon light.

Tugging at his collar, he slumped a little. He couldn't explain it, seeing as he couldn't make sense of it himself. All he knew was that he'd stood when he'd needed to and it hadn't hurt the way he'd both anticipated and grown accustomed to. He had expected excruciating pain. The kind that stole a man's breath and rendered him unable to speak, to breathe, to utter a cry for help. But it hadn't truly hurt.

"Ty?" she pressed.

"I don't know, okay? I wanted to stand up, so I did." He could add that he'd been desperate to identify the rider, that he'd needed to know why the cowboy had been riding so hard while Ty sat in his chair, worthless. Standing had been spontaneous, the results both exhilarating and terrifying. "You've seen me walk. What's the big deal?"

"The 'big deal' is that none of us thought it was so easy for you. We all believed you had excruciating pain and that's why you were clinging to the chair so hard." She sighed and, pulling her ponytail free, rewrapped the hair higher on her head. "What's going on, Tyson?"

He gripped the chair's armrests so hard the skin over his knuckles appeared bleached. "It's not that simple."

His barked response didn't faze Reagan. "It should be. If you're capable of doing more, then do more. Period. You need to get back to physical therapy. You need to stop sitting around doing nothing, letting your muscles atrophy. What you've been doing? It's giving up, Ty."

He jerked back and hissed at the sharp movement.

The reaction was instinctive but not necessary, because it didn't hurt. It wasn't comfortable, sure. But there was a world of difference between discomfort and *hurt*.

"Well, I'll be damned." Ignoring her, he wiggled out of his brace. Then, with a tentative touch, he traced the line of his surgical scar down his cervical spine. No acute pain.

"Ty?" Reagan pressed.

He glanced at her, jaw clenched. "I don't want to stand up." She started to say something, likely to protest, but he gripped the wheels of his chair and shoved them forward. "Don't confuse my not wanting to do something with me giving up. Two totally different things. Make sure you get that part straight when you tell Eli."

With that parting shot, nasty as it was, he rolled through the door and down the hall, forcing himself to consider sandwich condiments in lieu of soul-rattling comments. He'd take mustard over manhandling any day. And wasn't this embarrassing, his life reduced to sandwich analogies and defending himself to the ghosts of conversations present and past.

*Still doesn't mean either of 'em is right.*

He rolled on.

# 10

KENZIE HAD NO idea how far she'd gone before Indie slowed of her own accord. Lathered sweat lay in foamy patches along the mare's neck. Chest heaving, the animal slowed to a brisk walk, her head bobbing with pleasure at the hard run.

Knotting the reins, Kenzie rested them and then laid them over the horse's withers before lying down, her spine parallel to the horse's. A little hissing noise—air between her teeth—instructed the mare to drop to a far more casual pace. The *clop-clop-clop* of the horse's hooves on dry, winter-hardened ground sounded out a rhythm roughly one-fourth as fast as Kenzie's heart rate.

Somewhere nearby, cows called their calves to their sides, disturbed by the sudden appearance of horse and rider.

*Let them chatter. It's what parents do.*

And just like that, everything her dad had said to her raked across Kenzie's raw nerves again. Her shoulders twitched.

Indie shied away from the movement, the skin along Kenzie's back shifting hard in protest.

"Easy," Kenzie said, calm and firm, as she resituated herself in order to keep from ending up in the dirt. The walk to the barn would be a long one.

The horse snorted and tossed her head.

"You and everyone else, always with your opinions." She rubbed her wind-burned cheeks and stared up the darkening sky. The bone-chillingly cold air was infused with the crisp scent of snow. The sky would let loose before sundown. The cloud cover hung around like the wind's hired muscle, conveying to everyone that things were going to get ugly. It was only a matter of time.

As if in agreement, Indie kept her stalwart pace but made a wide circle that pointed them toward the barn.

Kenzie wasn't ready to return, but she didn't fight the horse's instinct when it came to the weather. Or anything else, really. She just hated the idea of facing the Covingtons right now, having to load Indie and all their gear and start the arduous journey home. And through miserable weather, no less. Just…ugh. But staying here wouldn't be an option. Not after today's confrontation with Ty.

She hadn't meant for it to get out of hand, but the opportunity to save face, to make the alleged partnership legitimate instead of a lie, had been too tempting. That whole "resistance is futile" thing proved true. Hurting Ty hadn't been anywhere on her impromptu agenda, but despite her good intentions, it had happened. The trust between them now fractured, she had no idea how to move forward. There would be no sidestepping the truth—that she'd tried to force his hand where it came to securing Gizmo's stud rights for the Malones' Quarter horse breeding program.

But he'd hurt her, too, when he'd said he'd sell off some of his stock. He would do it, violate that almost sacrosanct rule of keeping your best blood at all costs, simply to ensure he would be done with her. And that was what this was mostly about. The undisguised anger in his gaze had said he wanted her and her horse gone yesterday. After all, Indie was a mare. If he wasn't diligent in protecting Gizmo's honor, Indie may seduce him, get pregnant and demand child support.

"Such an idiot." Kenzie huffed out a breath, watching it condense on the air into a thick, white cloud. "We're not seducing his horse."

Really, though, did he hate her so much, think so little of her and her breeding program, that he'd go so far as to cull his own herd to satisfy the debt between them? She thought she'd been clear that simply allowing her to introduce Gizmo's genetics into her line would render the debt paid in full.

Ty's selling off a handful of horses he'd worked so hard to develop simply wouldn't do. There had to be another solution, one where they could both get what they wanted.

Drumming her fingers against one thigh, she didn't realize the wind had shifted directions and now blew straight out of the north. Since she was headed south, that put the thirty-mile-per-hour "breeze" at her back… and carried away any sound coming at her with an into-the-wind approach. Including that of the oncoming horse and rider. Kenzie had no forewarning other than Indie's sudden halt.

The mare raised her head, ears trained toward the stranger and unknown horse.

Scrambling to sit up with as much grace as she could muster, Kenzie reached out to grab the reins. She curled her fingers around the thin leather strips but couldn't stop herself from sucking in a sharp breath.

Her lungs promptly froze.

She'd been preoccupied, but not so much she hadn't realized the cold had been leaching into her and stealing what mediocre warmth she had left as the wind hammered her. The problem? She hadn't realized just *how* cold she'd become. And cold killed.

Eli reined in beside her, his mount a good deal taller than Indie. The man's furious stare pierced Kenzie with unabashed animosity. "What the blue blazes were you thinking, charging off into an unknown ranch like that with weather threatening to thrash us within the hour?"

That he thought to ride out here to make sure she was okay? She could almost call the action chivalrous. Almost. That he was railing at her the way a concerned parent would a small child? She couldn't, in good conscience, call that anything but overbearing. How typical.

Ignoring Eli, she nudged Indie into a swift walk.

Eli wordlessly wheeled his mount in beside her and kept the same pace.

"If there's something in particular you want, spill it," she called out over the now-howling wind. "Silent lawyers make me nervous."

"They should." He glanced at her before settling his Stetson lower over his brow to block the wind. "What's going on between you and Ty?"

There it was—the question she didn't want to answer, mostly because she didn't know how. She could offer a thousand speculative responses, but there was only one answer she had that would be accurate, though not terribly revealing. "Nothing." *Not at the moment anyway.*

"You claimed him as yours in the arena," Eli countered. "That doesn't say 'nothing' to me."

*Damn. He had to have an elephant's memory, didn't
he?* She was so tired of dancing around the truth, trying to make sure she kept her stories straight, that she
gave up and blurted out the truth. "We were friends
and, until the accident, occasional lovers. Nothing more,
nothing less."

Eli nodded, not sparing her a glance but rather seeming to file her answer away for future retrieval. They
rode in silence. The first snowflakes began to fall as
he spoke again. "Where does the partnership regarding
Gizmo come into play, then?"

She swallowed so hard she nearly choked. There was
no answer she could offer that wouldn't expose her as
a liar, nothing she could say that would absolve her of
the fact that she'd manipulated everyone in order to do
what Ty had asked of her, even if he didn't remember
asking. Painted into an uncomfortable corner, Kenzie
chose to say nothing. It was her best—*only*—defense.

Eli kept shooting short glares her way, waiting on her
answer. He finally snapped. "Look. I know you and Ty
are at odds. I get that. I'm not asking you to spell out
specifics, but I have to understand what you mean—or
meant—to him."

She twisted to face the man at her side. "What are
you talking about?"

"You raced by the house earlier."

"So?"

"That action got him out of his chair." Eli reined his
horse in front of Indie and stopped Kenzie and her mare.
"On his own. He got up and stepped to the window on
his own."

Torn between cheering at Ty's initiative and wanting to rage at the fact that he wouldn't do more for himself, she again defaulted to remaining silent. It was safer that way.

Eli glared at her.

She returned his stare without apology.

His curse was hot enough it should have melted the snow gathering on his hat brim.

Kenzie only arched a brow.

"You're baiting me, so I won't apologize for my language." He dragged a hand down his face, over his mouth, and then wrapped it around the back of his neck. Tension sang off his body. Sensing his anxiety, his horse fidgeted. Eli ordered the animal to settle. The command proved as effective as telling an alligator to go vegan. The big gelding wanted none of it.

"If you don't calm down, you're going to end up in the dirt," Kenzie offered with casual indifference.

"Probably." Eli relaxed his grip on the reins, settling his butt into the cantle before visibly forcing his shoulders to relax. "I'm just going to lay it out there, then. Cade and I are both sure you're lying about this whole partnership thing."

She sucked in a breath and the pervasive cold burned her lungs. Before she regained the ability to speak, and therefore respond, Eli pressed on.

"Problem is, we can't prove it. Ty doesn't remember anything from the point he entered the ring to the actual moment he woke in the hospital. You could make any number of absurd claims and there'd be nothing we could do to refute it." He shot her a shrewd glance. "That doesn't mean the absurdity of the claim will hold in court, mind you."

"Get to it already."

One corner of his mouth twitched upward before he forced it into neutral submission. "Cade and I talked about it, and I drew the short straw of discussing our plan with you."

"So far, you haven't discussed a dang thing," she ground out, her nerves so frayed she wondered they weren't sparking.

"We want you to stay and get Ty on his feet—"

"No." Her response was immediate.

"Not negotiable. In return, we won't challenge your claim to Gizmo's stud services. You'll get him, on your property, for ninety days." He rubbed his red nose. "We'll also repay you everything you've spent on my brother and his horse. It'll take us a while to figure out where the money's going to come from, but we'll make it work. With interest as well, though it'll have to be reasonable or the dude ranch will suffer." He did grin when he met her gaze this time. "Unless you're willing to take Monopoly money."

She huffed out a laugh, her breath condensing on the air. The snowflakes had become little beads of ice, pelting her exposed cheeks as the wind whipped around her. "I'm afraid I tried the Monopoly-money approach at age five after I broke one of my Dad's trophies."

"Yeah?"

"I tried to pay him off in pink bills and hotels. Ironically, he took it. I still ended up grounded for breaking the trophy when I'd been warned to leave it be." The memory was a fond one now that she could look at it through the lens of time and with the benefit of age. Her dad had been so serious, accepting her payment and then sending her to her room. He'd come up later and revoked riding privileges for a week after lecturing her on responsibility. Michael had sneaked her out twice in the following seven days to ride with him. Man, she'd loved him so much.

"Sounds as if you had a good father."

Kenzie's throat tightened. "I had... My family's amazing."

"Why the past tense?" Eli asked, openly curious.

"I lost my brother when I was a kid."

"I'm sorry." Eli reached out and fleetingly touched her arm, then withdrew. "I can't know the reality of losing a brother, but I do know the horror of thinking I lost one."

"Yeah." The word was little more than a breath lost to the wind's next gust.

"Stay, Kenzie. No matter the fight earlier, whatever you were to him hasn't died. That much is obvious."

"What do you expect me to be able to do that the doctors and therapists can't?" she demanded. "I'm the one person he's hell-bent on despising at the moment."

"Don't be so sure he despises you." He shot her an amused glance, his smile revealing dimples no woman should have to combat. "And you're a woman with resources. I doubt there's much you can't accomplish when you set your mind to it. Particularly where this man is concerned." He snorted and moved his horse a few strides away from her and Indie. "Let's just say the doctors and therapists don't hold the same type of influence over him that I'm willing to wager you do."

"You want me to—"

"Help him find himself again, Ms. Malone. You're the only one he's responded to, the only one he seems willing to engage with. Bring him back, not only to him-

self but to us. Please." When she didn't immediately respond, he pressed on. "Do this and...we won't contest
your *right* to Gizmo's stud services." He glanced up at
the sky. "Looks as if it's about to get ugly." With that,
Eli spurred his horse forward.

"The weather or this thing with Ty?" she shouted to
the eldest Covington's retreating form. He didn't answer,
so she shouted a second, more relevant question. "What
does Tyson think about this arrangement?"

If he answered, she didn't hear him. The snowstorm
had intensified to near whiteout conditions, Eli's silhou-
ette fading fast.

She urged Indie forward. The mare didn't need more
than a free bit, and she took off after the man and horse,
who were getting harder to see by the second.

ALMOST TWO HOURS LATER, Kenzie stepped into the one-
bedroom cabin she'd been given and shut the door. She
struggled out of her wet boots, her feet so cold they were
tinged blue. Next came the soaked jacket, and then she
started peeling off the jeans. That was when she remembered her last question to Eli: "What does Tyson think
about this arrangement?"

*He never answered.*

"Sneaky freaking lawyer," she muttered.

Tossing her jeans into the stacked washer-dryer
combo, she padded toward the bathroom on near-frozen
feet. She needed a hot shower to thaw out. Then she'd
reassess. The hardest part of the whole thing was that
it was a half blessing as well as a half curse. She'd have
to get Tyson to be vulnerable by doing the very same.

*How far can you take it without crossing the line
marked This Point is Too Far?*

She'd had a hard time living with the lies she'd told so far. What would it do to her to manipulate Ty into recovery? How deep an emotional marshland would she have to traverse to secure his buy-in? And finally, how many more lies could she—*would* she—have to tell to get out of this mess?

That was all disturbing enough. But a single question she hadn't been brave enough to ask hung around, nagging at her conscience, demanding its due.

At what point, if any, did she confront the feelings she and Ty had been so actively avoiding? The ones that had been coming to a head prior to the accident?

Fear choked her.

*What if he doesn't remember that, either?*

If she had to, she'd make him. Lord only knew how, but she'd find a way, because his reaction to what they'd had then said everything about how he felt about what they might have now.

*How do I make a man closely examine something he doesn't even want to glance at?*

The answer was so easy that she grinned. You teased a little. You made it desirable. And then you made it irresistible.

Outside, the worst storm northern New Mexico had seen in thirty years raged on.

It was nothing compared to the storm brewing in her heart.

ONLY HALF-AWAKE, Ty opened his eyes to find that the sunrise had set the world on fire, reflecting off the dazzling snow packed outside. He must have dozed off and left his curtains open last night. And he must have left the door unlocked, too. Because there was someone in his room.

Light created a brilliant nimbus around the individual. He blinked his eyes, trying to bring her into focus. Her? Yes, her. The swell of hips, the narrow shoulders and the outline of long hair pulled up in a sloppy topknot said she was female. She turned a bit. High breasts and a tight ass presented a tempting profile.

No, she wasn't "female." She was 100 percent authentic *woman*.

Below the covers, his cock stirred. He jolted, tipping his chin down as far as he could with his neck brace on but loose. How long had it been since he'd woken with his typical morning arousal?

"You awake?"

In the haze of half-sleep, he wondered for a moment if she was talking to him or his groin. "Has to be you," he mumbled, blinking faster.

"Who else?"

Grumpy tone or not, her voice glazed his skin and wound around his senses. Allure and sensual promise. That was what she was. He recognized it. Recognized *her*.

His cock shifted. Arousal crowded out everything but the memory of his hands on her body. Her response and his overwhelming desire to fill her senses and her mind.

*Her. It was her. She'd been responsible. Mackenzie Malone.*

"What are you doing here?" he rasped, throat dry from another night of sleeping on his back and breathing through his mouth.

"Came to check in on you."

His stomach did a lazy, nauseating roll. "I thought we left things pretty clear yesterday."

"They may have been clear for you, but I still have some things to work out. Besides, I can't leave now anyway." She gestured absently toward the window. "Snowed in."

Ty cleared his throat and half rolled, half flopped to a sitting position. Straining against his neck brace as much as he dared, he lifted his flat stare to hers. "I told you I'd pay you back."

"You really should know me better than that. I'm not worried about the money." With cautious steps, she moved to the edge of the bed.

"Then, what is it that has you so worried you're in my room at—" he looked at the clock "—barely six thirty in the morning?"

"May I sit?"

Before he could deny her request, his erection punched at the single-button fly of his flannel sleep pants. The damn thing would leap into her hands if Ty didn't keep it quarantined.

She noticed his physical reaction. Her answering smile revealed a single dimple. Years of knowing each other as intimately as they had created another private joke they would laugh over in the future.

*There is no future.*

Ty struggled to keep from shifting toward Kenzie as the mattress dipped with her slight weight. Their hips brushed. His erection strained toward her.

Eyes crinkling in unabashed amusement, she tipped her chin toward his lap. "I assume New Mexico has strict laws about keeping crotch creatures like that chained for the public's well-being."

He barked out a laugh. "Crotch creatures?"

She shrugged. "You have a better name for it?"

"As a matter of fact…" he started.

Kenzie waved him off. "Of course you do. Pretend I didn't ask." Twisting her fingers together, she settled her hands in her lap and trained her gaze on them.

The longer she sat like that, Ty wondered if he should prod her to say or do something. After all, she'd come to him. Then she spoke.

"I have a proposition for you."

Used to be conversations that started like that would have been full of promise. Now? Not so much. Anger burned through him, its heat far more brilliant than the sun on the pristine snow. "There's no point proposition-ing a broken man, Mackenzie. And in case you some-how failed to notice, *I am broken.*" The words lashed out with enough force they could have—should have—drawn blood.

Her chin snapped up, those fiery eyes blazing. "You aren't broken."

He chuffed out a bitter laugh and closed his eyes. *Instant anger—just add a dose of disabled cowboy.* "Right. Just go, Mackenzie."

"Don't know what I was thinking." She pushed off the bed, nearly toppling him over.

"Go easy there, Sasquatch," he muttered as he regained his balance.

Halfway to the door, she froze. Her steps were slow, precise and measured as she rounded on him. "Go. Easy." She arched a shaped brow with more sarcasm than had likely ever been conveyed by a single facial gesture. "You'd like that, wouldn't you? If I—hell, if *everyone*—went 'easy' on you." A wicked smile curled her lips up. "How long are we supposed to dance around you and your fragile psyche, Covington? What's the timeline here, because it's already getting old."

"What, you need to know how long you should pretend compassion?" The second he said it, he realized he'd pushed her too far.

Kenzie's eyes narrowed to furious slits. "Pretend compassion, is that what this is? When have I *ever* pretended? When have I *ever* been anything other than sincere with you?" She flinched, a shadow flitting through her gaze. He started to call her on it, demand an explanation, but she was already moving toward him with a hip-swinging grace any blues singer would have been proud to work. Closing the distance, she gently pushed him backward on the bed before crawling up his body like the lithe lover she'd once been to him. She braced one hand on either side of his head and leaned forward until their eyes met.

Heart in his throat, Ty reached up and pulled her hair loose so it cascaded around them. The thick curtain of waves hid them from the world. He tucked a rogue curl behind her ear. "What are you doing, Malone?"

"Making a point." With extreme gentleness, she slid her jean-clad core up and then down the length of his erection.

He hissed. "Which is?"

Leaning into him, she stopped with less than a breath between them. When she spoke, her lips moved over his. "This doesn't feel like the body of a broken man."

He began to breathe heavily, his eyes widening. "I can't do this."

She brushed a featherlight kiss over his lips. "At some point you've got to get back in the saddle, cowboy. Now's as good a time as any."

"Kenzie," he started, her name little more than a growl. "If this is about Gizmo—"

"Ty, your horse is in the stable. Leave him there." Slipping forward that last fraction, she claimed his mouth in a soul-stealing kiss.

She lit him up from the inside out. He was the sun to her solar system.

*Alive. Feel so alive.*

He ran his hands through her hair, reveling at its silky weight. Fisting his hand in her hair, he canted her head to one side and encouraged her to take the kiss even deeper, to give up some of the control she clearly struggled to maintain. The need to own the moment swept through him like a Chinook wind, melting the remnants of his heart's long winter solstice. For the first time in ages, he was warm. More than warm. Heat burned through him, chasing away the cold.

In her arms, Tyson Covington was reborn.

# 11

KENZIE BROKE THE kiss so she could simply look at the man beneath her. She touched his face, tracing a fingertip over his lips, up one cheekbone and then down. The hair along his stubbled jawline had grown out enough that it was on the verge of losing the prickly feel and becoming soft. She loved the way his hair was both light and dark. It was reflective of the man himself—the part people saw and the shadows he carried inside. She understood him. Probably more than he realized and definitely far better than he wanted her to.

He nipped the pad of her finger as she traced it over his lips again.

She instinctively pulled away and then pressed two fingers to his lips. When he kissed the sting, part of her relaxed. This was Ty. Simply Ty. He wasn't a stranger but a familiar lover. A man her heart recognized, craved, dreamed of more often than not. Looking at him now, it was as if she was seeing him for the first time all over again—the rush of attraction, the need to glimpse his smile, the desire to hear his laughter and, even more, to be responsible for it. Above all, though, was the yearning to touch him.

So she did.

Hands trembling so slightly she didn't think he'd notice, she reached out and undid the first Velcro strap on his neck brace.

Ty jerked away, eyes wide. "I can't take the brace off."

"Shh." The rip of the next strap seemed louder than the first.

"Seriously." His hand rested atop her wrist to stop her from removing the next strap. "Please, Kenzie. I can't do this."

She paused, taking in the undisguised fear on his face. "Can't or won't?"

He slid his hand to encompass hers and squeezed. "I don't..."

Cupping his face with her free hand, she pulled gently against his grip, giving him every opportunity to really resist, to stop her, to hold on to his fear and put it in front of his desire.

His gaze locked on hers and, eyes wide, he let his hand fall away.

She knew it was the ultimate gesture of trust. He'd handed over the keys to his fear, stepped aside and allowed her to rule the moment. No way would she abuse that. Moving with ultimate care, she pulled the third and fourth straps. Then she lifted the top of the brace away.

Fine tremors ran through Ty, transmitting his concern to her through every point where they touched.

Movements precise, care for the man tempering her hunger for him, Kenzie set the brace on the floor.

"I can't reach it," he said, voice strained to the point of breaking.

"You won't need it," she countered quietly.

"But what if I—"

"Enjoy yourself," she finished for him.

His brows drew together. "Huh?"

"What if you let your inner playboy loose and take a chance?"

He shook his head and froze.

Her heart stuttered. "Did you hurt yourself?"

"No," he answered slowly. "But what if I do?"

She closed the distance between them, feathering her lips over his in tiny kisses. "What if you *don't*?"

"It could happen, Kenzie. If I'm not seriously careful—"

"We'll take it slow." She pulled back a fraction. "Isn't the potential pleasure worth fighting through the fear? If we have to stop, we will. I swear to you I'll stop before I let anything hurt you, Tyson."

With slow deliberation, he threaded his fingers through her hair. "This is like losing my virginity all over again."

She grinned. "Why do I love the idea that I'm the one divesting you of your pseudo-innocence?"

"Because you have a very wicked side, Miss Malone." His smile grew and reflected in his eyes. "Coolest part? I've always wanted my very own Mrs. Robinson, and now I've got her."

Kenzie's laugh bubbled out, sultry and full of every unspoken promise she longed to make, from the generally innocent to the decidedly *not*.

*Mrs. Robinson indeed.*

Closing the distance again, she took the kiss deeper, angling her mouth over his so all he had to do was receive her. After a tense moment of consideration, he responded in kind. Hands searched, touched and learned; mouths tasted; tongues stroked and breaths came shorter and then shorter still. Here, in Ty's arms, no matter that she set the pace, she knew a sense of peace she'd been missing. She had longed for this, for him, ever since he'd walked out her hotel room door in the early morning on the day of the accident.

There had been moments, lonely and terrifying, when she'd wanted to leave Ohio, leave Gizmo in the vet's capable hands and go to Ty. But she hadn't. Hard as it had been, she'd honored his request that *she* see his horse well. Now that she had Ty, though, she wasn't about to let go. Not until someone forced her hand.

Those were thoughts for another time, though. This? This man tentatively coming to life beneath her? He was all that mattered.

His hot lips skated over hers, more demanding now than they'd been moments before. It thrilled her that he'd grown more brazen. She wanted both his capitulation and the masterful demands he typically made of her body. She wanted it all, to rule and be ruled, touch and be touched.

Her name was an invocation on his lips, a plea to her for something her conscious didn't quite understand but that her subconscious grabbed at greedily.

Kenzie ran her hands down Ty's sides, smiling against his mouth when he sucked in a breath. "Ticklish?"

"No," he replied, wiggling to get his shirttail out from under him and over his head. "Not even a little."

She dragged a blunt fingernail down his side, and he squirmed, trying to get away.

"Fine! Quit," he said, laughing. "I am ticklish. Now stop distracting me."

"What am I distracting you from?" she teased.

He looked up at her, face suddenly solemn. "I don't want to miss a single moment."

Pain blossomed in her chest, and for a second, she wondered what it was that could ache like that and yet make her crave more of the same. Then he cupped her breasts, gently rolling her pearled nipples between his thumb and forefinger. All thought turned to ash at the wave of desire that burned through her. Core aching, she moved to straddle his waist, to position herself to take what she needed.

His hands stilled. "Go easy, Kenzie."

"I promise. Just don't stop." She pressed her hands over his, encouraging him to manipulate the tender swells of her breasts with tiny squeezes of her fingers. "Please."

"I'll never deny you, baby." His hips surged when she pressed her sex against him, his groan the only thing soft about the moment. Or him.

She arched her back, one hand holding his to her breast while the other was parked on his thigh to help give her leverage as she rode him with a slow, hip-rolling motion. Drawn into the ageless rhythm, he gripped her thigh, pushing and pulling to help set the pace.

It had been so long, too long, since she'd been here with him. She didn't want to let the moment go, wanted it to last forever, but her body's needs were more immediate than her emotional ones. What her body wanted was achievable *now*. No reason to deny either of them the pleasure of connection and release.

Ignoring his wordless protest when she moved off his lap, she stood and stripped with perfunctory movements, more anxious to return to him than she was to make the action a seduction. The avaricious look on his face as his eyes roamed over her body said she achieved the latter regardless.

Kenzie crawled up Ty's body, stopping midway to untie his pants. She worked them down his hips and over his feet, tossing them clear of the bed.

With him lying before her without a stitch of clothing, she'd never been so grateful for the fit and finish the good Lord had bestowed on this man. He was beautiful, head to toe.

She could have looked at him for ages, explored his body and learned every peak and valley. Instead, she straddled his lap again, reveling in the heat of him against her sensitive skin. "No underwear. If you'd been in a car wreck, Tyson, you'd have scandalized the nurses."

He arched a brow at the same time he grinned, the look one of guileful amusement. "You know me, Kenzie—always ready and willing to play patient."

"You're incorrigible."

"Every man has aspirations. That one word sums mine up quite nicely."

Shaking her head, she leaned forward and nipped his earlobe. "Stop talking, Tyson." She didn't give him a chance to respond. With deft hands, she reached between them and positioned his arousal, then worked her way down his thick length. He stretched her. She reveled in the near discomfort his size caused. She hadn't been with anyone else who'd made her feel so much, made her long to embrace her sexuality and experience everything a skilled lover could offer. Particularly a skilled lover who knew her body so well.

In the past, he'd always seen to her needs first. Today,

though, she reciprocated his every touch, returned his every encouragement tenfold through words, sounds and intimate touches. He fought her at first, trying to make her reach the pinnacle alone. She was having none of it. Where she went, she ensured he followed. This was an exercise in mutual gratification.

She rode him with long, slow strokes, losing herself to the feel of him beneath her, the way his hips thrust up as she sank down, the way his deft fingers pulled her release to the surface, drawing it closer and closer with every careful manipulation. Her chest rose and fell, faster and then faster still.

Beneath her, Ty whispered her name. He dug his fingers into her hips and pulled her down his length as she sank low. His thrusts grew deeper, harder. The sounds of their lovemaking—the touch of skin on skin, the tender words and soft encouragements—filled the small room.

The fluttering of her release began to build, that intangible feeling that something huge was bearing down on her, something bigger than she could control, too large to define, too much for her skin to contain. The pleasure rushed at her suddenly and then over her, shattering her with brutal efficiency. She couldn't stop herself from bearing down on Ty and crying out, the magnitude of what he drew out of her too large for words.

Losing the graceful rhythm he'd kept, he gripped both her hips fiercely. Driving into her with thrusts so powerful he nearly unseated her, he followed her over the edge with a shout.

Kenzie closed her eyes and simply lived in the moment. No past. No future. Just the present existed. It was the only thing that mattered. She'd come too close to losing the chance to experience him even one more

time, to losing *him*, and she didn't want to go through
that ever again.

There had to be a way out of the mess she'd made, a
way to ensure everyone got what they most wanted—Ty
could keep Gizmo, the brothers could keep Ty whole,
and she…she could simply keep Ty.

TY LISTENED TO his heart. The act had become habitual,
the first thing he did every morning and the last thing
he did at night. He had to count out one hundred con-
secutive beats before he could do anything else. The
organ—muscle? Or would it be a morgscle?—tattooed
a repeating design against his rib cage. He forced his
breathing to slow as he discreetly checked his pulse.

*One sixty-four.*

Not a bad postexertion rate.

*Postexertion.* He grinned. *Postcoital, buddy. That
would be post*coital.

His bedroom rodeo queen shifted beside him. She
rested her head on his shoulder, her moist breath skat-
ing across his sweat-slicked skin.

Chilled, Ty fumbled for the edge of the quilt.

Kenzie sat up and pushed the thick fall of hair over
her shoulder. "Any reason you're manhandling the bedding like that?" She grabbed the edge of the quilt and
then paused. "Ty?"

He closed his eyes. "Leave it alone, Kenzie."

"Can't." She traced his stubbled jaw with the pads
of her fingers.

"I mean it."

"Still can't," she murmured. "It's okay to be angry.
It's also okay to admit you're scared. You suffered a hor-
rific injury. Makes sense you'd want to use caution as

you ease back into things." Her thumb drifted over the fullness of his lower lip. "What doesn't make sense is why you're so willing to accept suffering and settle for survival instead of fighting to live."

*She doesn't understand.*

His heart rate picked up speed, and Ty wondered that the morgscle didn't bruise as it threw itself against his sternum harder and harder. That would be bad in its own right, having a bruised morgscle. Fixated on the repeating thump of his heart, he started counting out the beats.

*One, two, three, four, five—*

"Ty?" She cupped his jaw.

*Shit. Have to start over.*

He pulled free of her touch.

*One, two, three—*

"Seriously, Ty." Completely unself-conscious, Kenzie moved to straddle his hips before putting a hand on either side of his face. "You have to slow down. You're going to have a full-blown panic attack if you don't."

"You don't get it," he said through clenched teeth, his nose flaring on each exhale and nearly sucking closed on every harsh inhale. "You don't know what it's like, Mackenzie."

"What *what's* like?" she asked with undisguised concern.

"You can't understand how it feels." He dropped his fist to his chest, daring that damn morgscle to defy him again, to fail to carry out its responsibility. "You haven't ever…" An invisible band around his chest began to crank down, cutting off his air supply and making his heart pound so loudly in his head he struggled to hear anything else. "I think I'm having a heart attack."

Her grip on his face tightened. "Look at me, Tyson."

He shook his head, two short, fast jerks of the chin. "Get off me. Go get help. Please."

"If I call your brothers, they're going to bring in paramedics. Given the remoteness of the ranch, you're going to end up with a Life Flight helicopter in your front yard and guests ogling the cowboy they've only heard about but haven't ever seen. They're going to airlift you to Amarillo where they're going to give you something from the benzodiazepine family of meds to get you to calm down."

"Move!" he wheezed. He pulled her biceps and twisted his hips, trying to move her.

No luck.

"First you have to look at me." The unforgiving authority in her voice demanded he comply.

Fear gripped him with all the fury of a pit bull after a fresh bone. All his life he'd been written off as someone who needed micromanagement, a dreamy-eyed kid with his head in the clouds and a quick smile that lacked substance. That stopped now. He was a grown man, and it was about time people started treating him like one. He'd survived more in the past two months than most people encountered in a lifetime, from the injury to the loss of memory to the pain of recovery. Resentment burned in him as he met her stolid stare.

"Tell me where you are."

"Under you."

One corner of her mouth kicked up. "Do you remember the last time you were there? It was in Fort Worth."

"I can't—"

She continued, talking over him. "You said it wasn't where you wanted to be then, either."

"Clearly, I was an idiot. Now move."

"Clearly." She stroked his hair off his forehead. "I didn't hurt you then, and I won't hurt you now." Continuing with the soothing motion, she talked. And talked. And talked some more. She told him about her favorite nice restaurant—San Francisco Steak House—and how she'd once driven seventy miles just to get to her favorite drive-through burger joint—Whataburger.

She told him how she'd had to argue with the salesman when she'd bought her last pickup truck because the man believed "a lady should never need four-wheel drive." That particular story had been delivered with several eye rolls.

She told him how she'd ended up getting drunk in college one night when she and some friends had gone bowling. She'd allegedly bowled the best game of her life—274—chomping on an unlit cigar and sporting a Hawaiian shirt she'd won off an elderly man on the neighboring lane. It was all alleged because she couldn't remember anything after the third game. And then she'd grimaced as she recounted the raging hangover the following morning.

She told him how she'd missed her senior prom because, even at seventeen, horses had mattered more than boys, and she insisted she'd never been as boy crazy as her friends had.

"Not until you met me anyway."

Kenzie smiled down at him, the look in her eyes no longer challenging but rather filled with humor and the warmth of good memories. "Sweetheart," she said as she waggled her eyebrows à la Groucho Marx, "you were never a boy." She leaned forward and gently nipped his chin. "You still drive me crazy, though."

His hands moved of their own volition, coming to rest on her bare hips. "Feeling's entirely mutual."

"What are we going to do about that?" The question, while delivered in a light tone, had a thread of seriousness woven through it.

He considered her, tracing his thumbs over the slight swells of her hips, letting them dip into the shallow depressions in front of her hip bones. "Hard to say. You going to keep talking me down from panic attacks?"

She lifted one shoulder in a casual shrug. "Why not? I can't do anything with the horses. Not until the snow melts anyway. How long does it usually stay on the ground?"

"Could be days, could be weeks. Never can tell around here." He shifted under her, settling his burgeoning erection against her core. "About the panic attacks—I suppose we'll have to work something out. You're a hell of a lot cheaper than my prescription."

He had the sinking feeling she would prove herself to be far more addictive, though.

# *12*

KENZIE COULD HAVE lolled around in bed all day without complaint, but there were chores to be done. With snow on the ground, it was all the more important that the animals were taken care of. She'd see to Indie and Gizmo, but she had no intention of doing it alone. Nope. If she had to hog-tie and drag him, Ty would come along.

Standing at the foot of the bed, jeans in hand, she considered the man lounging amid the rumpled sheets and wadded-up pillows. "You look thoroughly pleased with yourself."

"Darlin', what I just did is the equivalent of tagging a twelve-point buck with a single shot from a rickety bow sporting a crooked arrow less than ninety seconds into the first day of hunting season." Clearly proud, he hooked an arm behind his head. Propped up like that, he was the perfect picture of sanguine masculinity. His flinch wouldn't have been noticeable if she hadn't been looking for it.

"You okay?" she asked with intentional indifference, making it a point to focus on getting into her jeans and then searching for her socks and boots.

"Couldn't be better."

"Sore at all?" she pressed.

"In the best possible way."

*Gotcha.* She rounded on him, unable to tamp down her smile. "Awesome. Then, get up."

He stared at her as if she'd just gifted him with a wheelbarrow full of horse apples and expected gratitude for the fresh load of crap. "Get...up?"

"You can get down if you want to, but you'll still have to get up to do it."

"Funny girl." The teasing in his tone was still there, but beneath it ran an undercurrent of unease. "You're joking."

"Not in the least." She sank onto the bed and wiggled her cold toes into thick socks before reaching for first one boot and then the other. "I've got a ton to do today, and I need your help."

She could do everything on her task list by herself, and in fact she'd planned her day that way, not expecting company. But this little lie was one she could—*would*—live with, and gladly. She could even ignore the way her skin seemed to shrink a bit at the ease with which she prevaricated.

*Let it go, Malone. No harm, no foul.*

Standing, she grabbed a ball cap off the hook by the door and set about feeding her hair through the opening above the strap and then tightening it. "Didn't know you were a Denver Broncos fan," she said, pointing at the logo on the cap. Maybe she could get her dad to give up his fifty-yard-line seats. She and Ty could grab a Sunday-afternoon game, maybe spend the night in Denver and—

"Did you hear me?" he demanded, interrupting her mental weekend planning.

She glanced over her shoulder. "No. Sorry. What was that?"

"I said I'm not leaving the house."

She fisted her jacket in her hands. She didn't want to do this. Didn't want to fight with him, or to shame him or bully him into finding the motivation he needed to get off his ass and live again. She wanted him to want it on his own. The way he'd wanted her.

Setting her jacket on the corner of the bed, she crossed her arms under her breasts and faced him. "I don't understand."

"There's not much that needs explaining," he countered. "I'm still recovering, Kenzie. If I go out there, I could slip and fall, refracture my neck, damage my spinal cord worse than I did originally." He shook his head minutely even as he reached for his brace. "I could be hurt worse this time, maybe even paralyzed."

"'This time'?" Kenzie parroted, confused. "What do you mean, 'this time'? You planning on taking another header? Or maybe you intend to roll around in the snow with Gizmo and try to set a new world record for making snow angels while horseback. Wait. I've got it. You're planning a wrestling match with the colt in stall seven, aren't you?" She dug deep and retrieved a shallow smile. "He's not huge, but he's stout as hell. I wouldn't recommend it."

Color drained from his face and left his appearance pastier than Elmer's Glue save for two small bright spots that rode high on his cheeks. "You're just like everyone else. You're not *hearing* me on this."

"Oh, I hear you just fine. The difference between me

and 'everyone else' is that I refuse to kowtow to your temper tantrums or tiptoe around your irrational fears. I'm sick of this, and I haven't been around you even a fraction of what your family has. I'm not going to stand around and let you come up with any more excuses about why you can't do more than feed yourself pureed peas someone else fixed for you. This stops now, Tyson." She fought to keep from grinding her teeth as she decided just how hard to push him. At his mulish look, she pulled the emotional rip cord and let herself free-fall. "Put on your big-boy Pull-Ups and get out of bed already. You're freaking twenty-five years old."

"Twenty-six."

"What?"

"I turned twenty-six while I was in the hospital."

"And you think that fact—that you're older—works in your *favor*?" she exclaimed. "Did you fracture the logic center of your brain, too?"

He scowled at her, jaw set in a mutinous, hard line.

She pressed on, unwilling to give up the ground she'd made. "You proved you're man enough to get the job done—and more than once—this morning. Time to get that flannel-clad ass out of bed and back in a pair of Wranglers, cowboy."

"No." He pushed himself up, hands shaking as he tightened the neck brace's Velcro tabs. "You don't get to come in here like some…some…"

"The phrase you're searching for is 'knight in shining armor,' but that doesn't fit with your image of yourself, does it?" She spoke so low she knew he had to strain to hear her. Damn if she'd speak any louder. "Because then you'd be the damsel in distress. Truth is, you *are* the damsel on the railroad tracks in this little vignette.

But no one tied you down. There is no mustache-twirling villain to blame. There's only you. And now your private audience is throwing popcorn at you as the train bears down, yet you're just lying there shouting about the injustices you've been dealt. Get over it, Tyson. Cut the invisible ropes you've bound yourself with and get up already."

"Don't you stand there and pretend to understand what this is like for me."

"Oh, I don't have to pretend. I *know*. I've lived this before, Tyson. Always on the outside, but this is a familiar glass house." She grabbed her jacket and stormed toward the door, her throat burning with words she hungered to say but knew she'd regret, words she'd never be able to take back. She didn't want his pity, but she wanted him to understand that he wasn't the only one hurting. Not even close.

Spinning to face him, she clutched her jacket in one hand and yanked the borrowed ball cap off with the other. "I was thirteen when I saw my only brother killed in an accident eerily similar to yours. But it wasn't during a show. It was in the middle of an open-range branding. An exceptionally large bull calf got squirrelly. Michael roped him." She swiped at the single bead of sweat rolling down her temple. "But the calf fought, got wadded up in the rope. Michael's horse didn't have the experience to get out of the mess, and the three of them went down. Two of them got up. My brother wasn't one of them."

Wide-eyed, Ty opened his mouth and then closed it when she made a stop gesture with her hand. "Don't."

She'd achieved her goal—shocking him—with incredible efficiency. But the undisguised pity he didn't even try to hide proved more than she could bear. She felt the first emotional fissures open, the sensations not unlike someone dragging the tip of sharp needles along her skin. Superficial scratches that would provide weaknesses, places that would split with the right amount of pressure.

But the next words out of his mouth created a kind of emotional epoxy that bound everything together. "I'm so sorry. I didn't know. If I had..." He trailed off, his eyes closing as he fought to find the words.

She would spare him that much, at least. "How could you have known? You were fifteen. I wasn't even on your radar at that point, so it wouldn't have meant anything to you. Not on a personal level anyway. But my life was forever changed. Mom totally withdrew, first from her charitable and volunteer works and then from society altogether. It was as if she lost her will to live."

Ty's brows drew together in apparent anger. "I realize she lost her son, but she still had you."

He hit so close to the heart of her decade of hurt, becoming invisible in the shadow of a good man's death, that she took a physical step back. She couldn't go there. Not with anyone, but particularly not with him. How could he understand the consequences of Michael's death? How could he possibly grasp the fact that his love-'em-and-leave-'em approach felt very much the same to her? She couldn't. Not without turning those fissures into gaping wounds.

Instead, she pressed on. "While I pretty much lost Mom, Dad began wrapping up his rodeo career. He gave it all up so he could be there for Mom. So while I lost my mom's awareness, I gained my dad's time and attention. He turned that focus on me, on helping me become national champion." What she didn't say was that she'd followed that path for her father, stepping directly into Michael's boots. She'd never been able to fill them, though. Not for either parent.

"What about you?"

She whipped her gaze up to meet his. "What do you mean?"

"Just that. Your mom basically withdrew from life to grieve. Your dad gave up his career to come home and take care of your mom, but he also fought to keep Michael's memory alive by encouraging you to chase championship titles on the rodeo circuit. What did you do to grieve?"

Kenzie reached out and grabbed the edge of the dresser as black spots danced through her vision. "I managed."

"That's not what I asked."

Swiping at tears she was fighting not to shed, she cursed her own vulnerability. She hadn't want to show it to anyone, but particularly this man, who was notorious for running at the first sign of anything complicated.

*You wanted him up and moving under his own power? You're going to get your wish. This ought to have him hotfooting it out of the county by noon.*

That thought cut the last tethers of her emotional control. Fear and anger, thoroughly aged and seasoned by time, welled up and exploded out of her in a rush of almost unintelligible sound. "You want answers? Get your ass out of that bed. Better yet, make it to the barn and I'll give you all the intimate details."

"I don't think I can make it—"

"Then, ask for help. But bottom line? If you want answers badly enough, you'll find a way to get to the

barn. Come find me there, Ty." *Want me enough to try.*
"I'll answer your questions." *Need me enough to push
past the obstacles.*

Michael's death had left her with an aching loneli-
ness no one had ever been able to fill, partly because she
hadn't opened herself up to anyone enough to expose the
hurt she wore like a mantle every day. And she'd never
allowed anyone to get close enough that they might catch
even a glimpse of her most broken parts. She'd never
found anyone she trusted enough to understand her, to
understand the pain and the yearning.

Until now.

Ty understood. She just needed to get him up and
moving, to reinvest himself in his life and be active
again. He would emerge stronger. He just didn't know
it yet.

But she'd used her brother's memory paired with brib-
ery to get him to do it.

*Information.*

The thing it turned out he wanted most was information, and it was there, within his reach. He had only
to move, to walk, to make an effort and lay claim to it.
She'd set a beginning point—the bedroom—and an end
point—the barn. If he made it from one to the other,
she'd answer the questions he wanted to know.

But in the process, she risked her own emotional dev-
astation. Those fissures of grief would split, exposing a
dark abyss. When that happened, she'd survive only if
he was there for her.

She *needed* him to need her.

Ty LAY IN BED, his mind a roiling mass of thoughts and
ideas and realizations he'd failed to work out over the

years he and Kenzie had been first friends and then lovers. Just now, she'd thrown out what amounted to more than a double-dog dare—get out of bed to get the answers he craved. Then she'd fled the room as if all the regret in the world nipped at her heels. Seeing her inherent bravery stripped of fight, reduced to flight, wrecked him. That he couldn't give chase pissed him off.

"And just what do you think you'd do if you caught her?" he asked himself aloud. He'd like to think he'd rescue her from the heartache of her past, but in reality, there was no way to take the hurt away or undo what she'd experienced.

*And how do you think you're any different? Who do you expect to compensate you for what life's put you through?* his subconscious demanded.

Understanding drove the air from his lungs like a sucker punch. He was no different, and there was no compensation that would give him back what he'd lost. Not any more than he could return her brother to her or compensate her for his loss.

Which meant she was ultimately right. He'd been behaving like the proverbial damsel in distress, waiting on the hero to show up and rescue him.

Shifting to his side, Ty swung his feet off the edge of the bed, the momentum helping him lever himself up to a sitting position. Dark spots marred his vision and he blinked repeatedly. He'd been in bed too long, had spent too much time lounging. His muscles were almost useless, and his bones were so heavy they felt as if they'd been cast out of concrete. He wanted to lie back down and pull the covers over his head. How had he let himself go so badly?

Easy. Whereas he'd once lived large, life now scared him because it had scarred him.

His fingertips traced the four-inch knotty line of scar tissue that disappeared into his nape. The hair had finally grown back where the surgeons had shaved it in December. Strobe-like memories of the day of the accident drifted through his mind, mental Polaroid images he'd carry with him forever. Some were blurry, some were clear and there were others that were nothing more than black slides with no value. The brightest memories, though, were when he woke from the coma…and the night before it had all gone down.

He remembered everything about his and Kenzie's last night together. The smell of her perfume, the slip of the sheet that revealed one luscious bare hip, the passion, how she'd silently watched him leave the room—all of it was fresher, more easily retrievable than memories of his last phone call home. He lingered over the image of her lying in the tumbled bed, skin flushed and appearing well loved. He'd recalled that last image more times than he would cop to, no matter who was doing the asking.

The accident had messed him up, left him reeling as he'd fought to recover not only physically but, as she'd pointed out, emotionally. What he needed was to jump-start his life, to reengage on a more meaningful level. Raking one hand through his hair, he considered what it would mean to him to take over this alleged partnership. He'd have to get her to tell him…

*I'll answer your questions.*

There it was. His out. It was almost too easy.

He tightened his fingers and gripped his hair. She'd said it herself. If he made it down to the barn, she'd tell him what he wanted to know. What she'd failed to do was qualify the topics he could question her on. She'd left herself wide-open.

All he had to do was set aside the fears that were welded to his soul and then haul his broken backside to the barn.

# 13

ENTERING THE BARN after fighting knee-deep snowdrifts, Kenzie huffed out a sharp breath, watching as it condensed on the bitter cold air. This morning hadn't gone the way she'd expected. It was supposed to have been fun, full of her and Ty's signature teasing and laughter. The passion had proved too intense for that, though. And then her past had risen up and taken over the emotional bus, turning what had been a *Hope Floats* moment into a *Speed* film snippet complete with the bus going airborne, the crash landing imminent.

Grabbing a rake, shovel and cart from the equipment room, she set about cleaning the stalls she was responsible for. She started with Indie, hoping Ty would come in time to help with Gizmo. Her mare was quiet, absorbed with her grain ration, allowing Kenzie to work mindlessly as she replayed the conversation with Ty this morning, shying away from the hard parts.

She was nearly finished when she heard the sound that froze her where she stood. Booted feet. Steps slow and measured, the person entered the barn.

*He showed up.*

Adrenaline trilling through her veins, she set the pitchfork aside and stepped into the alleyway to find a cowboy she hadn't met emerging from the tack room.

He glanced up, seemed to recognize her, and his face shut down. All he said was "Sleigh ride for the guests," as he passed by, silently harnessing up a pair of draft horses before leading them out the opposite end of the barn.

Clearly, word about her "designs" on Gizmo had made it down the campfire gossip chain and made her persona non grata on the ranch.

"I swear," she muttered, scooping up another forkful of straw that needed replacing. "Men are far more active gossips than women." She glanced at Gizmo. "Present company excluded, but probably only because English isn't your first language." He nodded his head dramatically, and she laughed. "You're such a smart-ass."

She continued cleaning, the morning's conversation stuck on Repeat in her mind. She couldn't get it to stop, only to pause at highly relevant places or comments. Sweat trickled down her back, a ticklish, itchy line of irritation. Stepping over to the edge of the open stall door, she backed up to the corner and rocked side to side to scratch the itch. Her bra had dampened from the exertion, too. Glancing around, she shed her jacket and reached under her shirt to unhook her bra and wiggle out of it. Shoving it down the arm of her jacket, she tossed the garment on the nearest clean straw bale in the barn's alleyway.

"Better," she breathed.

Resuming her duties, she tried to ignore the building guilt that held down the trigger on her nerves. Movements jerky, she finally stabbed the shovel tip into the ground and leaned on the handle, closing her eyes. As pervasive as the cold was, it couldn't compare to the frost that rimed her emotional center.

*Can't believe I used Michael's memory that way.*

Exploiting her brother's death was wrong in a variety of ways, but she was far from the first to use it as a tool. Her mother had used it to get her father to quit the rodeo circuit. Her father had, in turn, used it as a manipulative tool to get Kenzie to take the professional rodeo circuit seriously, encouraging her to take over where Michael left off—"in Michael's memory," of course. Her maternal grandparents had used Michael's death to prod Kenzie into going to college because "Michael would have wanted it." Her paternal grandparents had suggested she could keep Michael's memory alive by riding with his bridle and reins in each event. At age fourteen, she'd balked, even cried, at the heartache caused by holding reins stained by her lost brother's sweat. They'd grown stern and told her how much it would have meant to Michael, as well as how much it *would* mean to her father, *their* son, to see that bridle worn in their grandson's memory.

The list went on; everyone from family members to friends to neighbors had exercised their right to gain what they wanted either for Michael or because Michael would have wanted it. She had despised them all for sullying her brother's loss that way, and yet here she was, finally succumbing to this warped expression of grief.

Only Ty had ever given her relief from the memories. He'd never asked because he'd never known, and that had suited her just fine. She could be normal with him, not the daughter/granddaughter/sister/cousin/friend who linked people to Michael's memory. She'd been Mackenzie Malone. Period. Sure, he'd known she was an heiress. But until the accident when he'd pleaded with her to save Gizmo, until she'd invested over one hundred thousand dollars of her trust fund money into saving Ty's horse and covering his medical bills, her money hadn't mattered. And for a few hours last night and this morning, she'd totally forgotten about the whole mess money and obligation and memories created. She'd just been Kenzie Malone in the arms of the man she loved.

She gasped. The man she loved…

*No. Not possible. She'd be a fool to fall in love with a man like Ty.*

Yet the longer she looked at what she felt for the man and what she'd done for him, the more she realized what a fool she really was.

She staggered across the wood chip–covered floor and crashed into the stall wall. Chest heaving, she shook her head and watched the fall of her hair move in slow, measured sweeps. And still, her internal argument carried on.

*Love? This isn't love. This is…something else. But not love. It couldn't be.*

How did she know, though? She'd never been in love. Not romantic love. Not spend-your-life-together-forever love. No. This couldn't be *that*. Not with Ty. She might have strong feelings for him, feelings so vibrant they marked her a neon idiot, but love?

"No," she whispered, thumping the edge of her fist against the thick wooden wall.

Her mind drifted back to the conversation she'd had with her father when she was only a teen. His words, so profound even then, had stuck with her.

*I don't care if the man you fall in love with is an artist, a pilot, a musician, a doctor or a garbageman*, he'd said.

He'd made absolutely sure she understood that the amount of money her potential spouse had—or didn't have—meant little to nothing, that her inheritance afforded her the means to choose a life partner based on love alone. How would her dad feel about Ty? Would he hold true to his word? He'd been proud that she'd managed to secure a partnership with Gizmo's owner, but also protective when he'd believed Ty was taking advantage of her. What would he think of her falling in love with that man?

"This isn't going to end well," she whispered.

Twisting, she leaned her shoulders against the stall and thumped her head against the wooden wall. How had she ended up here, of all places? She'd been struggling with her developing feelings for Ty even before the accident, but not once had she suspected they ran this deep. What would he do if she told him?

Probably grab his passport and disappear into a Brazilian jungle, she thought with an involuntary smile. But then he'd probably charm a young woman in some undiscovered native tribe and have to move on to Siberia when the respective father took offense to Ty's practice of short-shelf-life relationships. A small laugh escaped Kenzie at the thought of Ty being the only person with a tan in Siberia.

She'd be willing to bet he didn't sport tan lines, either.

That image led her mind straight back to a montage of memories, all of them centered around the myriad ways he'd pushed her body to new heights, had encouraged her to embrace the pleasure he could offer and then seen her to her own end before achieving his.

Her nipples pearled.

The response had nothing to do with the cold and everything to do with her cowboy. She couldn't let her need for him supersede his want of her. Not without consequence. But she hadn't been able to help it, hadn't been able to reject the psychological convenience of using Eli's promises as her excuse to see Ty.

In the quiet aftermath of lovemaking, when heart rates thundered and minds weren't quite clear, she'd been able to tell herself she was doing it to help Ty. It had also been a way to hoist her butt out of the sling she'd so efficiently parked it in with the very first lie. She could let Eli assume the responsibility of Ty's wrath over breeding Gizmo, get out of the partnership claiming that the ninety-day rights to the stud horse satisfied the debt owed, and she wouldn't have to tell her dad she'd made the whole thing up. If Ty was up and mobile before she left, even better for the Covingtons and her conscience.

A cold gust of wind curled around the door and stirred up straw motes. The pungent scent of animal grew sharper on the crisp, dry air. Outside, the merry jingle of sleigh bells and the hiss of wide steel runners over snow advertised the passage of the sleigh on its way to the chow hall to pick up guests. She envied them the view of the ranch, pristine as it would be. Nothing could beat the views from solitary vistas and the otherworldly quiet of snow-packed plains in either New Mexico or Colorado.

She longed to share a moment like that with Ty. They'd cover up with blankets and share a carafe of hot cocoa... Leaning her head back against the wall, she sighed and let her eyes drift closed. It would be idyllic. Except for the fact that Ty would know their driver. No fooling around for them, then. Maybe they could go out together, just the two of them. She'd driven a team before, and the smooth pull over snow wouldn't jar Ty's neck. He'd probably appreciate getting some fresh air and a firsthand look at the ranch. Heck, he might even enjoy taking the reins. If she could figure out who to ask… Maybe Eli? She'd get on that this after—

"You're fired."

The deep voice shocked her out of her romantic reverie. She shoved off the wall and spun toward the voice, knocking the shovel over in her haste. The handle snagged on the side of the stall trolley with a wood-to-plastic *thwack* that made her wince. But it failed to dislodge her heart where the stupid organ had welded itself to her larynx and wasn't giving up ground.

"We Covingtons run a tight ship, Ms. Malone. Daydreaming isn't allowed."

A slow, sensual smile on familiar lips made her knees weak.

Ty tipped the brim of his hat up, those mirth-filled dark eyes ringed with even darker lashes peering down at her. "Unless, of course, you were thinking of me. Then, I'll not only keep you, I'll see that you're promoted for exercising stellar judgment and exceptional taste."

She should have issued a witty reply, should have told him she didn't work for layabouts, should have said… something. Anything. But all she could focus on was the last sentence.

*He'd keep me.*

Throat inexplicably tight, she knew with the certainty that darkness always yielded to light that her grief had yielded to hope. Somewhere in the recent past, at a time she hadn't been wise enough to recognize, her heart had tipped the scales from "like" to "love" where this man was concerned. It changed nothing because he didn't know. Not yet. But for Kenzie?

It changed everything.

TY WATCHED KENZIE struggle through a string of emotions, her eyes darkening even as the color leached from her face only to come back in a rush, her cheeks flushed and rosy. Her eyes didn't lighten, though, and he wondered what had gone through her mind. Half of him wanted to ask while the other half shied away from anything powerful enough to steal the voice of such a straightforward woman.

"Why are you looking at me like that?"

"You came," she said. How she packed two simple words with so much weight he'd never understand.

"I did."

"I didn't think you would." She rubbed her nose and glanced away. "Not really."

"I wanted the answers you promised me."

Her shoulders sagged a bit. "Fair enough."

"You okay?"

"Fine," she said, the lie evident. She met his hard stare, but her gaze lacked the emotion that had filled it only moments before. "Great."

"Liar."

"Prove it."

"You promised to answer any question I asked if I hauled my bedbound backside down here. I did, so hold up your end of the bargain."

Her short bark of laughter could have shattered glass. "Sure. Let's get right to that."

"I'll ask again, Kenzie, and don't feed me some line of bull. Are you okay?"

"I've been better and I've been worse." She shifted her gaze to the stark white landscape, squinting as the sun reflected off the smooth surface of the snow. "This morning was full of surprises."

*Michael.*

He should have realized discussing her brother's loss would leave her a little raw. "Look, about that. I'm truly sorry."

She offered him a shallow smile. "Sure. Thanks."

Setting that aside because he wasn't sure what to do with it, he couldn't help but poke at her a little. "So which is it? Are you fired, or you moving up the food chain here at the Covington family dude ranch?"

She started to answer only to stop, clear her throat and start again. "Did you actually say, 'I'll not only keep you'?" she deadpanned. "With lines like that, it's a wonder you Covington men aren't single forever. 'I'll not only keep you…' Idiot."

He laughed, the sound stirring the horses and bringing large heads over stall doors. Except for Gizmo. Kenzie had left his stall open as she worked. Now the grullo stud nudged her aside as gently as a twelve-hundred-pound animal could and made straight for Ty.

He had dreaded this moment for months now, truly facing Gizmo again with nothing between them. Heart pounding brutishly and with no finesse whatsoever, Ty fought to ignore it all—the heart that beat too hard, the sweat itching between his temple and hat band, the giant animal he'd loved from birth, the way his neck ached a bit without his brace, the woman watching it all.

The horse stopped in front of him, those pale, long-lashed eyes considering Ty with wisdom far too vast for a horse. He nodded his head in short, slow movements, a silent demand of sorts.

Ty raised a trembling hand toward Gizmo.

The horse stepped into the touch. Dropping his head, Gizmo pressed his broad forehead into Ty's chest and let loose a sigh of heartrending contentment.

Ty swallowed repeatedly, trying to force down the emotion that flooded his throat, alternately squeezing it tight and filling it so full he couldn't breathe. His eyes burned. Damn if he'd cry, though. The only tears he'd shed over this whole thing had been shed in private, and he wasn't going public at this point. No way.

Instead, he gritted his teeth and raised both hands, resting one on each side of Gizmo's face. "Brought you something."

The horse didn't move.

He leaned in closer. "Candy."

Gizmo raised his head and then, without warning, reached out and pulled Ty's hat off his head. With a toss worthy of a California beach bum spinning a Frisbee out over the sand, the horse launched Ty's hat to the side before beginning to mouth the pocket on his shirt.

Ty felt it happen before he could control it. He burst out laughing. Digging out the Blow Pop, he unwrapped it, used his pocketknife to snip the stem and offered the confection to the horse.

Gizmo snatched it up, bit down and grunted, nostrils flaring. Flicking his tail, he chewed and chewed, the crunching unnaturally loud. Then the treat was gone and he was nosing at Ty with more intent.

"One more, you giant addict, but then I'm cutting you off." Ty pulled out a jumbo-size Tootsie Roll, unwrapped it and broke it into three pieces. He fed them to Gizmo one at a time.

As if he understood this was it, the horse savored these more, actually drooling as he chewed.

"I take it no one fed his sweet tooth," he said quietly, running his hands all over Gizmo's face and neck.

"That is…" Kenzie gestured to the horse and then to Ty. "He's addicted and you're his dealer. I mean, you realize that, right? And I *did* give him sweets, just not quite as many. I mean, sugar cubes and apples and—"

"Sugar cubes are child's play and apples don't count."

"I did the best I could." Her voice was stiffer than her spine, which was poised to shatter.

He realized then that she'd taken his teasing as criticism. That hit him harder than having stirred up her old grief. He needed to keep things light between them, needed to ease the pall that seemed to hover over her like a dark cloud. "Darlin', you know I'm yanking your chain." He glanced around. "So what was it you wanted my help with?"

She watched him closely, her gaze guarded. "You up for it?"

He wasn't about to admit he was wearing down, and fast. He needed to get the answers he'd come for. "Bring it on."

"I'll put these tools away. You get Gizmo back in his stall." She retrieved the pitchfork and tossed it into the little trolley.

"And then?"

"Then you're going to drop your drawers. The rest should be pretty self-explanatory."

Tyson stood stock still for a split second. "You going to inoculate me?"

She grinned, but the gesture was off. Her words, however, weren't. "Not exactly. But if you want to be patient to my nurse, that's fine with me."

Mouth dry, he struggled to issue the command that would direct Gizmo to return to his stall. Took two tries, but he managed.

"Hurry up, you giant slug," he whispered harshly. "Your buddy here has a date with a cowgirl-cum-nurse he hopes will be even half as naughty as she just sounded."

He shut the door behind the horse and latched it before slowly facing the interior of the room…and Kenzie heading toward him. The look on her face was impossible to interpret, divided as it was between forecasting personal injury and powerful pleasure. But when she caught him staring, she smoothed her features and blinked slowly as she licked her lips.

Something was clearly wrong. He wasn't sure what it was, wasn't sure she'd own it even if he pressed. The one thing he knew, could relate to, was the mind's desire to cede control of the issue to the body's ability to find a simpler solution. Whatever hurt she bore or anger she harbored would be soothed by this, this thing between them. And her reaction in this, her need for him, was the part of her he understood with startling clarity because her needs mirrored his—for touch, taste, companionship, comfort, home. *Each other.*

He reached for his belt buckle long before she was within arm's reach.

# 14

KENZIE GRABBED THE front of Ty's jacket and pulled him into her.

*One more time*, she silently pleaded. *Just give me one more time with him, and then I can live with the consequences.*

She would do her level best to control the moment, to give only enough of herself that Ty wouldn't realize what she felt for him. She would take as much as she could so she would have the memories to dole out to herself a bit at a time for the rest of her life. It would have to be enough because she had no alternatives. Not until Ty made his move anyway.

He pulled her into his arms on a self-satisfied sigh. "You're like an addiction, Mackenzie. One I can't seem to get enough of. I come down from the high you create to find I'm already craving my next hit." He pulled her even closer to his body so they were pressed thigh to thigh, belly to belly, chest to chest. "And I want you to hit me again."

Her laughter wasn't as light as she intended. "Never

ask a woman you've recently irritated to hit you, Tyson. Not without at least qualifying the request."

He pulled away and looked down at her. "I'll take whatever you dish out, woman. No complaints."

A hard shock coursed through her, head to toe, and she jerked in his embrace. *He doesn't mean that, has no idea what he's saying.*

Brow furrowing, he stared at her with undisguised confusion. "Problem?"

No answer would have sufficed. Instead, she tightened her grip on his jacket and ran her other hand into his hair before pulling him back to her. "You talk too much."

"Yeah?"

"Yeah."

"Then, shut me up," he whispered, the heat of his breath scalding her chilled skin.

A slight pull against his head and their lips met and their mouths fused, welded by the power of their passion.

Kenzie took what he offered and demanded more, taking his mouth with a proprietary sense for which she refused to apologize. She wanted as much of him as she could garner, as much as she could claim without scaring him. Was she selfish? Yes. But was the behavior necessary? Even more so.

Passion flared between them, the sound of his quickening breath and her hammering pulse drowning out all but the sharpest sounds. She experienced him without reservation, memorizing the smoky flavor of coffee on his tongue and the pinewood smell of soap saturating his skin. The well-worn flannel shirt beneath his jacket had pilled after so many washings and created a rough texture underneath her fingers. Almost panting, the sound of his desire escalated in her ears until she matched him breath for breath. Then his arousal punched at the zipper of his jeans, its heat juxtaposed with the cold shock of his large belt buckle.

Slipping her fingers under his waistband, her nails gently scraped the head of his erection.

His hips thrust forward, pushing more of him into her hand.

Smiling, she ended the kiss—for now—and backed across the barn. "Awfully anxious for a man who had sex less than two hours ago, aren't you?"

"You're responsible for this, Malone." The growled words were almost pained.

"Then, step it up, cowboy." She slid her fingers deeper into his boxer briefs. "Stop dragging your feet."

"Where are we going?"

She tilted her chin toward the tack room. "I'm about to show you a new way to ride."

His eyes nearly bugged out of his head and he lurched forward, all but knocking her over in his urgency to get them both through the doorway.

The door crashed open on the dimly lit room. Smells of leather and saddle soap, both familiar and comforting, saturated the room. Everything here was well organized. Saddles for the guests perched on numbered wall pegs while the larger saddles used by the Covingtons and the ranch's cowboys were all stored over oak barrels that had been mounted length-wise on short legs. Each saddle's stirrups and cinch were flipped over the seat. Bridles and reins were hung on shorter pegs, the name of the horse printed above the headstall. There were bits and pieces of leather as well as spare equipment parts in different bins. Buckets filled with currycombs, sweat scrapers, hoof picks, hoof oil and more lined the bare wood shelves. It looked like so many other tack rooms but still had the feel of the Covington place to it—organized but exuberant, profitable but still fun.

Kenzie intended to stick to the fun part, if nothing else.

Leaving Ty standing with his back pressed to the closed door, she located his saddle and wordlessly moved toward it.

"I can't ride." The croaked admission came from Ty with such little force the words almost didn't make it to her.

She spared him a quick glance before setting to work cinching the saddle to the barrel as tight as she could get it and adjusting the stirrups so his feet would clear the ground. "Everyone has to get back in the saddle sometime, baby."

"Kenzie, I…" He cocked his head and considered her actions. "I'm mounting a *barrel*?"

"Only so I can mount *you*," she said as casually as if she'd offered him the day's weather forecast.

Crossing to her, Ty paused at the saddle and considered it. When he didn't move any farther, she patted the tooled leather seat. "Nothing's changed about this in hundreds, even thousands of years. One leg up and over."

"Right. Because people ride barrels all the time." Though the words were liberally seasoned with humor, his eyes were solemn.

"Fine. We'll go about this backward, then." She turned the little space heater up and then locked the door. With a mocking sigh of despair, she shucked her boots and then shed her layered tops. The heater wasn't keeping up, and goose bumps broke out over her skin.

That didn't stop her, though. She stripped out of her jeans before stepping back into her boots. Rounding on Ty, she realized she'd never felt more cherished, more wanted than she did right then. And it was all due to the look of unadulterated hunger on his face. Hunger *she* had put there.

"Lose the boots and jeans, cowboy, and then park that fine ass of yours in the saddle, feet on the floor," she said, voice husky. "I'm not telling you again."

"You don't have to." He kicked his boots to the side, pulled his jeans and briefs off and crawled into the saddle. A little yip of shock escaped him when his bare butt hit the cold saddle leather. "I trust you're going to do something about this cold?" he said through clenched teeth.

It took her a moment to form an answer. All she could think was that he looked like every cowgirl's dream, sitting there with his cowboy hat tipped up, his flannel shirt pushed back over his hips and framing his arousal, that firm rear propped against the saddle's cantle, muscular legs flexing as he pressed the balls of his feet against the wood floor. He was the epitome of male beauty and the manifestation of feminine desire.

Moving through a haze of want, she let her feet carry her to him. She planted her hands on his chest and gently pushed.

It was a testament to his trust in her that he leaned back, never checking how far he'd have to go before he met security.

When his shoulders touched the wall, she drew a deep breath. "Hands on the skirt, grip the edges."

He followed her commands, gripping the leather skirt

on the saddle and curling his fingers into the fleecy underside.

"Lock your elbows." She waited for his compliance before issuing her last directive. "Don't let go until I tell you to."

"Bossy little thing," he murmured. Then he went silent, watching with wide eyes as she stuck one booted foot into the shortened stirrup and swung her opposite leg over the saddle—and his lap—to park that foot in the other stirrup.

She ended up in the saddle backward, facing him and straddling his lap. Bracing her hands on the wall, one on either side of his head, she leaned in to kiss him— small, teasing nips that drew groans of frustration and approval from Ty. Rolling her hips back and forth resulted in a delicious sexual tension as her sex rubbed over the underside of his shaft and drew even deeper sounds from him.

Kenzie deepened the kiss at the same time she managed to slide the tip of Ty's arousal home, slowing sinking down his length until she took him all the way to the hilt.

Ty let his head fall back with a shout. He reached for her, but she slapped his hands away.

"Hands on the skirt or this stops. Now."

He glared at her, dark eyes wild. "Don't drag this out."

"Impatient much?" she teased.

"Kenzie…"

She rose as high as she could without losing him, and leaving one hand on the wall and gripping his shoulder with the other, she took him in again. Moving with controlled grace, she rode him hard, leaning forward to whisper in his ear all the things she'd dreamed of doing

with him, to him and for him since they'd been apart.
She was graphic.

He obviously didn't mind.

She rode him harder as the wave of pleasure grew
within her, taller and wider and so dense it blocked out
all thought, all reason, all sensibility.

"Let me hear you, baby," he ground out, clearly fighting to hold out as long as he could.

That wave of pleasure crested, hung suspended for
the briefest second before crashing down and dragging
her under. He was her point of reference, her anchor, her
true north in all matters of the heart. She hated him for
it as much as she loved him.

And love him she did.

He followed her into the abyss, seemingly willing to
drown with her.

She buried her face in his neck and mouthed the one
thing she most needed him to know and most needed to
hear in return. *I love you.*

That she couldn't say it aloud infuriated her. She was
better than that.

Sitting up, she knew she had to tell him, even if for
no other reason than he should hear it before they talked
about where they'd gone wrong. He deserved the truth.
She took a deep breath at the same time he reached out
and ran two fingers down her throat and paused between her breasts.

He looked up, a sea of emotion churning in his gaze.
"Kenzie, I... You need to know that I..."

She held her breath. If the Fates were fair in any way,
he'd tell her first, would admit his heart was hers.

He glanced down, coughing to clear his throat. "I
never thought this would be so hard."

"Go on," she encouraged.

He gave a short nod. "Sure." When he looked at her, the depth of his emotions hadn't changed, but the flavor had. "There are things I have to understand, questions only you can answer."

She all but fell out of the saddle, fighting not to run for her clothes.

Her heart sang him a love song; his couldn't even manage to hum the chorus in tune because he wasn't interested. Answers meant far more to him than anything else.

That was when she knew she'd never get what she needed most from him.

Love.

Ty LEANED AGAINST the tack room wall, the rough wood of the planks snagging loose strands of hair as he sagged. It was cold in the little tack room, but it wasn't totally miserable thanks to the small portable heater they ran in the heart of winter to keep things from shrinking. He tilted his head back and grinned into the darkness of the high ceiling. The heater had done its job for him, too.

*No shrinkage here.*

He loosed a soft chuff of laughter. Even though the words were issued internally, he found the testosterone-fueled pride in them funny.

Glancing at Kenzie, he watched her gather her clothes, her back to him. No need to keep up appearances if she wasn't paying attention, so he leaned more heavily against the wall. Gravy, but he was worn out. He hadn't had this much sex *before* the injury. Not that he was complaining. No way. The reality that he wore down so quickly was just discouraging. For what seemed like the hundredth time this morning, he mentally slapped himself for letting his physical conditioning get so far away from him.

*I totally pulled the tied-to-the-tracks damsel in distress routine. Crap. I hate it when she's right.*

"What are you scowling at?"

Kenzie's rich, sexy-as-sin voice coiled around him. If voices were ranked for seductive powers, she'd be in the ninety-ninth percentile. It just didn't get better than her voice in the dark. He pulled a fleece saddle pad off the wall and settled it over his lap in an attempt to hide her effect on him. Miserable failure as far as the effort went.

She raised her brows in mock disbelief. "Eli's not old enough to be hunting down little blue pills, so where'd you get one?"

"I don't need one any more than he does." Indignation, thy name is wounded male pride.

"You certainly don't, but that?" She gestured to his reviving erection. "That's not normal. Not even for you."

He huffed out a short laugh. "What do you mean, not even for me?"

"Easy. You're a total hound. You've been without sex for more than two months and you obviously needed to burn off the excess drive. But seriously? Three times in as many hours?" She grabbed her jacket and stuck her hand first down one sleeve and then the other before emerging with her bra. "That's damned impressive for a twenty-six-year-old."

"You're not suggesting I'm too old to hold my own? And did you just pull your bra from your jacket sleeve?" He scrubbed a hand over his face. "I don't remember putting it there."

She chuckled, her hair hiding her expression as she

bent forward at the waist and hooked the band behind her with deft movements. "Long story, but I took it off before you got here."

"Why?"

"Like I said, long story." She slipped into her body shirt and then retrieved her flannel.

Then what she said hit him. Not the little bits and pieces. No, it was the core of her original statement. *You're a total hound. You've been without sex for more than two months and you obviously needed to burn off the excess drive.*

Did she really think so little of him? Worse, did she think what had happened between them was nothing more than a quick romp to burn off excess sexual energy? Something suspiciously akin to shame burned through him, and he didn't like it. At all. Tugging at his collar, he let his gaze roam the room. He tried to focus on the condition of the other cowboys' gear. He stared at the shelf with the hoof picks and short cans of hoof oil. He made a mental note to get more of the heavier oil on hand for the remainder of the winter. He considered the state of the room and the fact that it likely hadn't been cleaned out since before his accident. But his mind, for all he tried to avoid it, kept winging back to her statement.

Parking his feet in the stirrups, he grabbed the saddle horn and pulled himself upright. His back and neck ached. The muscles along his spinal cord objected to his repositioning, screaming and shaking in exhausted protest.

*Whatever.*

What she'd said, the assumption she'd made about them, reignited the fear he'd been harboring since she showed up in his room early this morning. Part of him knew he was being irrational. Things had always been casual before, so why wouldn't they be so now? But the other part of him, the part he rarely allowed to come out and play, was reeling at her dismissive attitude. Before he considered the consequences, before he weighed the pros and cons, he simply asked the thing he suddenly most wanted to know. "What's this about, this whole sexcapade, this morning and again now?"

She twitched as if she'd been bitten by a horsefly.

His stomach plummeted. "Mackenzie?"

Focusing her gaze anywhere but on him, she worked to hastily button her shirt.

"You missed the first one." That his proffered observation was so calm startled him. No, he'd never been one to lose his temper, to strike out when hurt. But this was a familiar hurt under unfamiliar circumstances. His mind swung open the doors of his past and suddenly he was four again and remembering his earliest experience with rejection. His father had refused to teach Ty to ride because he was too "flaky." The old man had insisted Ty keep his feet on the ground until his head was out of the clouds and he learned to be more practical where the animals were concerned. He'd deemed Ty's affection a weakness. He'd rejected Ty's love.

So Eli had taught him to ride. His old man had instead taught him not to overinvest in emotion that could be used against him.

He'd done just that, though, by letting Kenzie know how much Gizmo meant to him. He'd created and exposed his own Achilles' heel when he'd begun to wonder if there could be something more between him and the woman across from him.

And she'd used that weakness to her advantage. She'd exploited him when he was down and out. She'd positioned herself perfectly to get her hands on the only thing he'd guarded more carefully than his heart.

His horse.

It was a stupid thought to fixate on, but his mind dogged it like a border collie on a belligerent steer, herding it closer and closer until Ty remembered his dad's exact pitch and tone, his articulated disappointment in the dreamer Ty had been and the voiced expectation of Ty that really boiled down to his dad having no expectation at all. It had been the first time Ty had realized that who he was might not be good enough.

While his dad was long gone, he experienced the same realization now, that he wasn't good enough for this woman. His value came from what he possessed, not who he was.

Floorboards creaked as Kenzie shifted foot to foot, anxiety bleeding from her like a grievous wound.

"Answer me," he said quietly, all traces of the dreamer in him gone.

"Ty," she all but pleaded, her voice soft, wrecked even.

A world of hurt was delivered with that one word, one syllable. "You told me you'd answer my questions if I came down to the barn. I'm here. Hold up your end of the bargain, Malone."

Chewing on her lower lip, she silently wrapped her arms around her middle. Hands restless, she finally fisted her shirt's loose flannel, clutching it so tightly her knuckles bleached out. Still, she stared at the floor and refused to look at him.

The longer she stalled, the more frantic his imagination became in filling the silence until he couldn't take it anymore. His worst fear manifested itself in a burst of terror-driven accusation. "You don't want me. You're not here for *me* or my recovery and well-being. You're only here to protect whatever bullshit arrangement you crafted that would let you get your hands on Gizmo."

Her chin snapped up. Eyes wide, she spoke in a whispered rush. "I didn't talk you into anything."

"I might not remember the accident, Kenzie, but I *know* I didn't offer to partner with you." Chest heaving, muscles weak, he still forced himself to kick his feet free of the stirrups, swing a leg over the saddle and stand. He wouldn't square off with her sitting down like some invalid.

"You don't remember! There's no way you can be sure."

His stomach plummeted at her desperate attempt to turn this back on him. He wasn't having it. "I may not be sure, but you have no proof."

"I have my word."

"If you did what I think you did, your word's not worth anything anymore, Mackenzie."

"What are you getting at, Ty?" she choked out.

"Did you lie?" he demanded. When she didn't immediately answer, didn't offer a vehement denial, he thought he might be sick. Swallowing convulsively, he asked again. "Did. You. Lie?"

"Yes," she whispered.

"What?" The question exploded from him on a broken gasp. His heart plummeted. Unreliable thing that it was, the muscle-organ didn't bounce when it hit the inner heel of his left boot.

The damn thing shattered.

# 15

INSTINCT URGED KENZIE to salvage the situation, to explain why she'd done what she'd done, then make it right between them. One look at Ty's face, though, and she knew with absolute certainty that that was no longer an option.

Fury slowly bled over his countenance, replacing the raw, unadulterated shock of her initial admission.

She'd always intended to tell him the truth. Every day that passed had made it harder, though. Her realization only an hour before that she loved this man had totally thrown her and scattered her good intentions to the four corners. Understanding and despair collided in her and left her reeling, exposed and terrifyingly vulnerable. Worse, she'd been a fool, had never expected him to call her out like this, to use her promise to talk about Michael to garner an admission of guilt from her. "Ty, I—"

He sliced his hand through the air, cutting off her explanation. "Don't." Breathing so hard he was nearly panting, he gripped his shirt and yanked it away from his chest. "Just…don't."

She stepped closer, hand outstretched. "Are you having a panic attack?"

His movements were almost spastic, uncoordinated even, as he pushed off the wall and shuffled toward the barred tack room door. Shoving things out of the way with total disregard, he wrenched the door open and gasped, breath condensing on the rush of cold air. "You don't need to pretend anymore."

Her mind slowed, comprehension warped by the tendrils of panic spreading through her. "Pretend?"

"I get it, Kenzie. Your dad's been after me for more than two years, trying to get me to stud Gizmo out to the Malone Quarter horse empire." He barked out a bitter laugh, and she recoiled. "You know, I just realized that's about the same time you showed up in my life." He shot her a hard look. "Was that what this was all along? An attempt to get me to fall for you so I would sell Gizmo's baby batter to you? Because you realized you couldn't beat me in genetics otherwise?"

Kenzie stood still as death while inside she figured she more closely resembled a crash-test dummy—arms akimbo, head at an odd angle, one foot twisted the wrong way. She should answer him. She knew that. Yet words eluded her, refusing to coalesce into any semblance of coherent thought. Her mind was a landfill of expired good intentions and discarded hope. So she stood there, silent, and bore the wrath of the man she would have done anything for—had done *everything* for—cringing when his smile grew brittle, hard but breakable.

"I think the worst part of this is that you used my memory loss to your advantage to gain the thing you wanted most from me. *Gizmo*." He spat the horse's name like a vile curse. "He's all that mattered to you. And the second you saw an opening, you took him under the guise of a false partnership."

"I saved him," she objected.

"You saved him so you could use him," Ty countered.

"I did what—"

"What you wanted, Mackenzie," he shouted.

"What you asked me to do!"

His grin was colder than the wind chill at the peak of the Sangre de Cristo Mountains. "See? I can't dispute that because *I don't remember.*" His voice had been cold, but his eyes suddenly became glacial. "And that's why you brought Indie, isn't it? You intended to breed her to Gizmo while proximity wasn't an issue. Nice, Kenzie. Real nice."

She met that desolate gaze head-on. "No." After months away with Gizmo, she'd simply wanted her horse's company. She'd needed to be able to ride when she wanted to and without asking for the equine equivalent of a Hertz rental car. But her response didn't matter. All Ty was willing to see was the worst possible interpretation of what she'd done and why.

Jaw knotted, skin pale and lips almost nonexistent in his face, Ty stared at her, unblinking. "I want you to pack whatever's in that cabin, get your gear and your horse out of my barn and get off my land before I call the sheriff."

Kenzie straightened at the threat. "And just what are you going to report, Ty? That the woman you've been sleeping with off and on for years spent over one hundred thousand dollars on you and your horse, and she screwed you senseless this morning?"

One corner of his mouth curled up, the expression uncharacteristically cruel. "No. I'm just going to report she screwed me."

She'd expected heartbreak to sound like a gunshot. It

didn't. There was a very quiet internal fracture, a tiny gasp. Then came the onslaught of pain, an emotional riptide that pulled her under. It stole her breath. It darkened her vision. It wrapped tentacles around her chest and bore down. It hurt more than anything ever had.

"Get off my ranch, Mackenzie, and don't come back." No steadier than the town's resident drunk on a weekend binge, Ty stumbled out of the tack room and out of the barn.

By the time Ty made it to the house, the fear of falling had surpassed "probability" and moved straight to "inevitability." That was why he didn't shout when he collapsed in the foyer. He couldn't *sit* up, couldn't *get* up, so he simply lay there and fought to catch his breath.

The door opened, exposing his clammy skin to a blast of outside air. He shivered, silently fighting through the additional discomfort it caused. Screw that. It hurt. *He* hurt. All over. He rested his forehead against the hardwood floor and groaned.

"What the…" Cade's large hands ran over his back and arms, searching for injury. "Talk to me, Tyson," he ordered, voice gruff. "Tell me what happened."

"Life. And don't go soft on me. Not now." Using arms and legs weaker than a newborn foal's, he fought to roll himself over. Cade tried to help, but Ty uttered a sound suspiciously growl-like, and the larger man backed off. "I'm not a freaking damsel," Ty said through gritted teeth.

"Damsel?" Cade said, confused. "I'm at a loss here, man. What does a damsel, or being one, have to do with you being sprawled out on the floor?"

*Irony, you're a real bitch.* "Everything. And nothing." If it wasn't so painfully true, he'd have laughed. If only…

Using the last of his reserve, Ty managed to roll over.

Cade tried to help him sit up, but Eli chose that moment to open the door. Caught unprepared, Cade was shoved forward. Ty had to give credit where credit was due, though. His older brother managed to throw himself clear of Ty's semiprone form, presumably in an attempt to keep from crushing him.

"What are you two pony jockeys doing crouched in front of the door?" Eli demanded absently as he dumped his wet boots into the boot tray.

Ty cradled his face in his palms and batted his eyes at his eldest brother. "Oh, you know. Hanging out. Discussing fashion trends and the latest *E! News* gossip. We were going to use the living room, but furniture is so passé. It's all about casual living now."

"Smart-ass." Eli looked Ty over. "You fall?" he asked quietly.

"Flat on my face."

"Break anything?"

*My heart.* "No."

Eli offered Cade a hand and then the pair turned to him. "Let's get you up, then."

As a unit, they worked to help him to his feet and continued to support him until they made it to his room and perched him on the side of the bed.

Cade pulled Ty's boots off and Eli helped him get laid down on the bed. Ty ignored the soft scent of perfume on the sheets.

*Kenzie.*

Ty struggled to sit up. "I need to change my bed before I lie down."

"You're worn out, Ty. Leave it for now," Eli answered. "We'll handle the sheets later, when you're up to it."

He couldn't stand it. "I want the sheets changed. Now."

Eli faced him with slow deliberation and arched one brow. "Do I look like Cinderella?"

Anxiety rose within him. Fighting to draw a slow breath, to calm himself down, Ty considered his options. He didn't want to admit that the smell of her would make him crazy, didn't want to own the fallout, the fact that he'd been had. Lying here with her scent surrounding him, though? Totally worse.

Chucking pride aside, he looked first at Cade and then Eli. "Mackenzie Malone lied." That was, apparently, all it took to free the words he'd held in check. He dumped the whole story at his brothers' feet, starting with how he'd first met Kenzie and ending with him walking away from her less than an hour ago. Nothing was left out. Nothing was off-limits.

When he finally finished, Cade and Eli were quiet. He didn't understand. He hadn't expected them to grab their ropes and scout the tallest tree for a hanging, but neither had he expected them to hold their opinions to themselves. They were all opinionated. Always had been. Rule of thumb said they were also brutally honest with one another under every circumstance. Nope, he didn't get their silence at all.

"She lied. She admitted it." He rubbed at the crease between his eyebrows. "So why do I suddenly feel like a total dick?" Shifting around in bed, he adjusted his pillows and looked first at one brother and then the other. The way they both avoided eye contact sent up his internal "shark in the water" flag. "What did you guys do?" No answer. He pushed himself higher up his headboard. "One of you will tell me or I'm calling the women in."

"No need for that," Cade said, sinking to a crouch beside the bed.

Ty rustled up a teasing smile. "Chickenshit. Emma's a total softy."

His older brother quirked a brow, the gesture speaking volumes even though all the man himself said was "Keep telling yourself that, little brother."

Eli pulled up the room's only chair, dropping into it as though he bore the weight of the world on his shoulders. He still wouldn't look at Ty.

The action, or inaction, seasoned his brothers' hesitation with discomfort and flavored it further with guilt. He was about to call them both on it and demand answers when Cade finally broke the silence.

"You have to understand, Ty, that we thought we were going to lose you, first physically—" he reached up and pinched his upper lip hard enough to turn it red "—and then emotionally." Blue eyes met Ty's brown ones. "You checked out on us after you came home. None of us in this house were willing to risk losing you, either physically or mentally."

Ty stared at the other man. "When you did you go all Dr. Phil on me?"

Cade didn't bat an eye when he answered, "When it seemed to all of us that you'd stopped caring whether you lived or died."

He flinched. "Well, that was about as subtle as a kick in the nuts."

Cade exploded off the floor, at eye level one minute and in Ty's face the next. "You want subtle, discuss the nuances of fine wine with Emma. From me you get the hard truth, little brother." He grabbed Ty by the front of the shirt. "There's not one of us who wouldn't have done worse than we've done if it meant saving your sorry ass when you were too broken to do it yourself."

Blood rushed through Ty's head at a frenzied rate, the swooshing white noise so powerful it almost drowned out the sound of his voice in his head. "What have you done?"

Cade looked over at their eldest brother.

"Answer me," Ty shouted, startling the two men and bringing Emma racing into the room.

"What happened?" she demanded, breathless. Her gaze traveled the room and came to rest on Cade's ruddy complexion. "You told him."

Ty zeroed in on his future sister-in-law. "They haven't told me anything."

She joined the rank and file, fixing her gaze anywhere but on him.

"Emma. Please." He didn't remotely regret the pleading in his voice. Every second that passed left him feeling sicker, more certain he'd somehow committed the worst mistake of his life.

Emma moved to stand by the side of the bed, edging Cade out of the way and, at the same time, placing herself between Ty and Eli. "Get out."

"This is between us, Emma." Eli's admonishment was soft yet firm.

"I would have respected your position if you'd admitted everything when you and Cade first concocted the idiotic plan. But you didn't. Now you're refusing to tell him what you've done because you don't have the guts to own your mistake."

"I would've thought you'd have learned from that," Reagan said from the doorway.

"I did." Eli stood and faced his wife. "He's my baby brother, Reagan."

"He's a *grown man*, Eli. You and Cade have to stop trying to keep life from happening to him." The brunette closed the distance to her husband. "I'm with Emma on this. Get out."

Cade crossed his arms over his chest. "What are you going to do?"

"What you two should have done from the beginning," Emma answered. "Give him the truth." Cade opened his mouth, no doubt to argue, and Ty watched Emma shut the big man down with a single look. "If you'd owned this before, I'd have kept out of it. You didn't, which means Reagan and I are going to clean up the mess you two have made. We don't need your help—"

"Or your blessing," Reagan added.

"To do it," Emma finished with a nod to the other woman. "Respect me on this, Cade. I told you that you and Eli were wrong to try to manipulate Kenzie."

Ty forced himself to sit up. "Come again?"

"Out. Now," Reagan said, her tone brooking no argument, and yet it was compassionate for all that.

His older brothers left the room. Eli was pulling the door closed behind him when he paused. Staring at the floor for a moment, he seemed to need to work up the courage to face Ty. When their eyes met, Ty's breath seized in his chest at the sheer remorse on Eli's face. "I'll ask you to remember one thing. We did this because we weren't willing to lose you. Nothing, *nothing*, is worth that."

Then he closed the door.

Side by side, the women Ty loved like family faced

him. And what they told him upended everything he thought he knew.

But he'd been right about one thing.

He was a total dick.

# 16

BETWEEN WHITE-KNUCKLED driving conditions, pulling a trailer over snow-packed roads, changing a flat tire halfway home and trying to figure out how to break the truth to her dad, Kenzie was ready to drop long before she saw the sign announcing that Cheyenne Wells, Colorado, was seventeen miles ahead. She took the next exit, crossed under the Malone gate and began the last leg of her journey home. Winding her way across the ranch, she let herself take in the sweeping grassland and strong five-wire fences that ran to the moonlit horizon. It was a good thirty minutes of dirt roads, muddy potholes and creative curse words before the mare barn came into view.

Parking out front, she rested her forehead on the steering wheel, the only sound that of the engine ticking as it cooled. Eyelids heavy, she may have passed out for a minute before jerking upright at the rap of knuckles on the driver's-side window.

She powered the glass down with a touch before shutting the engine off. "Hey, Andy. You're up late."

"Could say the same for you."

She couldn't stifle the jaw-cracking yawn, only nodding in response.

The weathered cowboy leaned back and made a show of examining her truck and trailer. "Looks as if you drove through every snowdrift and salt spill you could find."

"They treated the roads pretty heavily for ice so it wasn't too... You know, I was going to say it wasn't too bad, but that's a bald-faced lie." And she was done with those. For good. Even if it hurt, it was the truth or nothing from now on.

Opening the door, she hopped down from the cab. "The salt needs rinsed off, but it'll have to wait until tomorrow."

"That's a first."

"What's that?" she absently asked.

"You puttin' off caring for your precious truck." He shook his head and grinned. "You two ought to write your love story down for future truck owners, Mackenzie. I'm stuck in a mediocre relationship with mine, and you give me hope I might just find 'the one' if I keep searchin'."

She felt the color leave her cheeks. Such a profound statement given what she'd left behind earlier today.

*Roll with it, Malone.*

Dredging up the last of her emotional reserves, she managed a small smile. "Funny guy."

"Suppose only a fool gives up hope, though, huh?" Andy slapped the halter lead he held against his leg. "Came out to check on Bean's labor."

Impossible as it seemed, Kenzie perked up. "Bean's foaling?"

"Said so, didn't I?" Andy glanced over his shoulder. "The Malone's in there with her now."

Her knees simply folded and she went to the ground.

Andy dropped the lead and went to one knee beside her. "Malone," he called, low but strong.

"No," she croaked. "Don't call him."

"Too late." The cowboy stood and slipped into the darkness at the same time Jack Malone appeared.

Her dad sank to a crouch beside her, running his hands down her arms. "What's hurt, baby?"

*My heart.* "Nothing." *I'm bleeding out.* "I'm fine, Dad."

"You're sitting on the ground, your skin's the color of chalk dust and corral slop is soaking into your jeans. And from the sounds of it, your horse is protesting being left in the trailer." He reached out and gently removed her hat. "Talk to me, Mac."

The use of her nickname made her throat tighten. It was the name Michael had bestowed on her when he'd found out their mom had dared deliver him a sister instead of the brother he'd requested. Michael had refused to call her "a girl name," and Mac had stuck.

"I'll get your mother." Her father made to stand.

"No," she all but shouted as she reached out and grabbed his arm. A single tug pulled him off balance and down he went, landing with a squelching sound on the ground beside her. "Please."

The look of surprise on the infamous Malone's face eased the tension in her, but not as much as his comment did. "You're going to be the one to tell your mother later why I had to go—what's it called when you don't wear underwear beneath your britches? Commandeering? Soldiering?" His face brightened. "Going mercenary!"

She laughed as heat infused her cheeks. "You have to stop with the modern slang, Dad. It's called going commando, and no, I don't want to tell her why you're going to shuck your underwear in the barn."

He reached over and yanked on a piece of her hair. "You just landed me on my ass in the muck, kiddo. It's soaked through my Wranglers and my unmentionables are now soggy. I'm ditching 'em as soon as I can. I think there's a pair of clean coveralls in the barn I can pull on."

She plugged her fingers into her ears and began to chant, "La, la, la, la." Then she met his amused gaze. "I'm not pulling my fingers out of my ears until your lips stop moving."

He grinned.

She dropped her hands. "I'm ruined. You realize that, right? No daughter needs to know these things. As far as I'm concerned, you and Mom are Ken and Barbie."

"I don't get it."

"You have no defining—" she blushed furiously and waved her hands about "—*parts*, Dad. *Parts*."

His booming laughter was answered with coyote chatter, their yips and barks carrying across the night breeze from who knew how far away. Wiping away tears, her dad grinned down at her. "Ken and Barbie. Does that make you… What was that teenage kid's name?"

"Don't," she said, smiling. "Don't even try to remember Skipper's name, Dad. You'll ruin childhood memories by renaming her something like Petunia."

"Fair." He reached out and tucked a loose strand of hair behind Kenzie's ear. "You never were much for dolls."

"They weren't—"

"Horses. I know." His smile was wistful.

She suddenly felt as if she were five again and the world, *her* world, was centered right here on Malone land. Leaning over, she rested her head on her father's shoulder. "I needed that, Dad. Thanks."

"What's going on, baby girl? Talk to me."

"What makes you so sure anything's going on?" She was stalling, but she couldn't help it.

"Don't bullshit a bullshitter, honey."

She nodded, fighting the wave of nausea that rose up her throat. "I want to..." Resting a hand on her chest, she forced herself to meet her dad's open gaze. "I should to talk to you before I see Mom."

"Sure." He whistled and Andy reappeared. "Do me a favor and walk Kenzie's mare out and then put her up."

"Sure, boss." Andy moved with bowlegged agility, unloading the horse and moving away with her before Kenzie could summon an effective protest.

Jack Malone turned to her. "So spill."

She sucked in a breath and held it to a slow count of ten before letting it rush out on a harsh exhale. Every cell in her body was screaming at her to flee, seeming to understand this was a fight she'd never be able to win. Fighting down the urge, she rose, moved to the wooden corral fence and scrambled up to the top rail, where she perched, waiting for him to join her.

Her dad followed, standing in front of her with a suspicious look on his face. Crossing his arms over his chest and widening his stance, he took two deep breaths and schooled his features. "Go on, then."

If she was going to deal in hard truths, she might as well start with him. She'd spent her whole life trying to please this man, but never more so than over the past decade. Not once had she felt she'd succeeded. What she had to tell him now would irrevocably cement her sense of failure. She'd survived a lot of crap over the years, but she wasn't sure she could survive this.

Her dad considered her, then closed the distance between them. Reaching out, he gently took her hand and cradled it in his own. "You know there's nothing you can say or do that will make me stop loving you, Mac, so out with it. What's been eating at you?"

"I lied to you." *Nice finesse, Malone. Nothing like hurling it at him via fast-pitch.* The truth hung there, suspended in flight. It had been offered and, apparently, received, and neither sender nor recipient was sure what to do with it.

He finally offered a short nod. "Okay. About what?"

She'd known from the moment she got into her truck and headed home twelve hours ago that she would have to tell him everything or nothing. There would be no CliffsNotes version.

"You won't stop loving me." A declarative question if ever there was one.

"There's nothing in the world that could make me stop loving you, Mac."

*Then, everything it is.*

Decision made and reassurances offered, there was no point in stalling. So she didn't. Starting with the admission that she and Ty had been lovers, she ran through the entire course of events, wrapping up with the details involved in her long trip home.

There was only one topic she didn't address: the fact that she'd fallen in love. That in the midst of the continual heartache involved in healing physical wounds and the terror of learning to recognize her true self, she'd fallen in love with Tyson Covington.

There would be fallout from her actions and the choice to keep this one fact to herself. It was one of life's simple truths—cause and effect. A Japanese man had even created a kind of chart—an Ishikawa diagram—to make results traceable and repeatable and to identify weak points. Whoever Ishikawa had been, he'd no doubt have a heyday with her psyche. She was so messed up she probably would have broken the initial diagram. Hell, she'd probably have broken the theory *behind* the diagram. Whatever. All she wanted right then was her dad's reassurance that it was all going to be okay.

The longer she waited, the longer she stared at Jack Malone's neutral countenance, the more her internal panic levels escalated. They were fast approaching DEFCON Total Emotional Annihilation when he finally spoke.

"Why lie, Mac? I was proud of you for doing the right thing for the right reasons—helping someone in need, helping someone who couldn't take control of a horrifying event." He parked his fists on his hips before exhaling through his teeth. Staring at a point on the ground somewhere between them, he quietly asked, "Why lie about any of this?"

Mackenzie nearly came out of her skin when the answer came from behind her.

"Love makes a woman do crazy things." Stella Malone, Kenzie's mother, stepped out of the shadows, climbing the fence to sit next to her daughter. A look of contrition decorated the older woman's face, emphasizing the fine lines that good makeup and bright smiles usually hid.

Kenzie glanced between her mom and dad, confused. "When did you come down from the house?"

Stella's shoulders rose and fell with feminine grace. "When I heard your father laughing. He rarely laughs like that. I wanted to know what was happening and be part of it." She reached out and took Kenzie's grimy hand. "Appears I got here a little late."

"I'm glad you came," Kenzie managed before the first fat tear broke over her lower lashes. She rubbed at it with undiluted aggression. "I'm so sick of crying over this. It seems as if that's all I've done all day." She drew a shaky breath and, clutching her mom's hand, forced herself to lift her face to her father's. "I'm so incredibly sorry, Dad. I didn't mean to do anything more than secure the right to save Gizmo like Ty asked me to do. I know what it's like to lose your hope." Her voice broke, and she had to clear her throat before continuing, "I didn't want that for Ty. Beyond that, I don't have any excuse for my behavior."

Her dad simply stood there, his chin tucked to his chest, refusing to meet her eyes. When he spoke, his voice had dropped two solid octaves and gone gravelly. "Do you love him, Mackenzie?"

"Does it matter?" The question could have been rhetorical. It wasn't. And her parents knew it.

"Get on up to the house and get cleaned up. I want you to stay with us for a few days." Spinning on his heel, he started for the barn.

Her mother's hand tightened around hers.

"Does it matter?" Kenzie asked again, louder this time.

Jack Malone answered without slowing, without turning around. "It changes everything."

THE SUN WAS going to melt Ty's brain. That or it would cause the useless gray matter to spontaneously combust given the level of alcohol he had consumed last night. He rarely drank and never to excess, but last night had been his major exception. There was no doubt he'd come close to pickling his organs.

A pitiful groan sounded from somewhere near the foot of the bed.

Ty stretched one leg and was met with a flexible but solid object.

The toe punt resulted in a muffled, "Ow. Quit it." Bedding rustled. "Man, you have the bluntest toes. They're like little battering rams."

Ty blinked slowly, forcing his eyes to adjust until he managed to squint in the face of certain death. His mouth was so full of cotton he expected he could have spun yarn straight out of it.

*At least then I'd do something useful with my piehole.*

"What happened?" a different, deeper voice asked.

*Cade.*

Ty lifted his head, shocked at the volume the drumming between his ears immediately escalated to. *Wow*, he mouthed, gripping his temples. "Shh." At the hissed command, the invisible musicians banged harder on their drums.

If they were within reach, he'd pinch their little heads off.

*Bastards.*

As if it were their fault.

*Why am I thinking of them as sentient beings?*

Refocusing, he realized Eli had crashed along the foot of the bed while Ty had ended up crossways. He rolled over, and the entire room pitched. He slammed his eyelids closed, gripped the edge of the mattress and swallowed repeatedly. Bravery didn't return to him for several minutes. He hated throwing up.

When the worst of the spinning nausea passed, he chanced a peek through half-slit lids to find Cade curled up on the floor. The larger man had fallen asleep again, but he wouldn't stay that way. Sunlight crept across the floor with every progressive tick of the clock's hand. In less than half an hour, Cade would be hit full in the face with the morning sun.

Ty squinted harder. "At least I won't suffer alone."

The aroma of fresh-brewed coffee crept through the room.

He groaned his appreciation.

His brothers responded in kind.

He tried to grin but his face almost broke, and the drummers in his head went wild.

"Rise and shi— Hell's bells, boys." Reagan sounded choked. "It smells like a bar down here."

A booted foot crunched over what he assumed were peanut hulls, adding a thundering bass line to the chorus in his head.

"What did you three do last night?" she demanded.

Ty threw an arm over his face and mumbled, "Tried to figure out women. Apparently the answer does *not* lie at the bottom of a bourbon bottle. Who knew?"

Eli must have moved because the mattress shifted. "No shouting. Have a little respect for the dead."

A soft feminine cough preceded a second woman's voice. *Emma.* "Cade?"

"What Eli said. Dead. No shouting."

Emma laughed softly. "You know, I figured you'd cut yourself off before it got this bad."

"Would have, but there's apparently a man code. I got my card last night," he answered, a little pride woven through the evident misery.

Ty blindly held out a hand. "I'm not married to you or getting married to you, so I get coffee first."

"Why?" Eli groused, sitting up and cradling his head with a pained look.

"Because you, my brothers, are going to get feminine sympathy. I'm going to get—"

"Your ass kicked," said a stern male voice he didn't recognize.

His brothers staggered to their feet and put themselves between him and the door.

*Always with the saving me. Kenzie was right. I'm the freaking damsel of the Covington clan.*

The thought of her ripped the painful wound of the truth open all over again. He'd drunk to forget. Apparently, "amnesia in a bottle" was temporary and not only caused physical hangovers but provided a sustainable fuel source for emotional ones.

Gripping the iron headboard for support, he rose to his feet. One look at the man in the doorway was all he needed to realize the shit storm that was about to rain down on him. "Good morning, Mr. Malone."

# 17

THERE HAD BEEN heated words, shouted accusations and one very creative threat involving an electric cattle prod that left Ty fighting the urge to look behind him with every step away from the house he took. Total chaos had ruled for several minutes until Reagan had loosed a sharp whistle that had nearly rendered Ty and his brothers deaf, mute and blind as their skulls shattered.

Jack Malone had scoffed at the three of them. "For your sake, I hope you don't always expect to find the solution to your problems in the bottom of a bottle." With that, he'd spun on his heel and started down the hall, heading for the front door. He'd paused there, gripping the doorknob. "Get yourself cleaned up and meet me in the barn, Covington."

"You ask for one, you're going to get all three of us," Cade had responded, the low, slow words as clear a threat as if he'd handed the older man a formal challenge.

"I don't do threats, young man. You should remember that." He'd stepped into the brilliantly clear, brutally cold day. "I'll deal with Tyson alone or not at all." It would have made sense for him to slam the door. That he'd shut it with controlled care expressed his anger far more effectively.

"Crap." Ty sank to the edge of the bed. "I'm not up for this."

"It's my fault." Eli sat next to him and leaned forward, resting his elbows on his knees and his forehead in his hands. "I'll deal with him."

"No."

They all peered up at Emma.

"This is Ty's mess." She'd glanced at each of them in turn, her gaze coming to rest on him as compassion paired with the hidden hard-ass in her. "I love you, but it's time you started cleaning up after yourself."

"Told you," Cade muttered, the corners of his mouth twitching.

Ty rose again, forcing himself to stand without hanging on to anything...or anyone. "You're right." He glanced around the room. "Anyone interested in checking out my junk when I get dressed should stay. Everyone else? Out. I'll deal with this."

And that was where he was now—headed to the barn to find out what particular pound of flesh Jack Malone had come for.

The snow had been cleared between the house and the barn, but the downhill trip still proved exhausting. Getting home was going to suck. Picking his way into the big building with careful steps, Ty was forced to remove his sunglasses to peer through the barn's dim interior. "Mr. Malone?"

The man stepped out of Gizmo's stall. "Wanted to see what my daughter's money paid for. Appears it was to save a fine horse and an irresponsible man. Seems that would give her fifty-fifty odds of making sound financial decisions with her inheritance in the future, wouldn't you say?" He didn't wait for an answer, instead turning his back on Ty dismissively as he shut Gizmo's stall door and continued to look over the horse. "He's a beautiful specimen."

"He's not a 'specimen.'" Ty knew Malone was provoking him, knew better than to let the man get to him. But that he'd basically reduced Gizmo to nothing more than a sperm factory really pissed Ty off. "'Specimens' are found in petri dishes, Mr. Malone. Gizmo is both my companion and business partner. He's also going to provide the next big genetics push for the breed." Ty tilted his Stetson back and crossed his arms over his chest. "You're well aware of that or you wouldn't have been working so hard to breed three of your mares to him."

"That's fair." Malone shifted and propped an elbow on the stall door. "But let's be honest, Mr. Covington. You'd have to sign over exclusive breeding rights to the Malone ranch if you ever thought to reimburse my daughter for the financial investment she made in you and your 'business partner.'"

Ty's stomach hit the dirt and started digging, because apparently ground level wasn't sufficient for how far his stomach intended to fall. "I want to be clear here, Mr. Malone. I always intended to pay her back, with interest, for the investment she made in me and my horse."

The infamous rodeo cowboy pushed off the door and strode across the hitching area toward Ty, his steps sure, his temper brewing. "Damn skippy, you will."

"The dude ranch is mortgaged, but we're realizing a healthy profit. While I can't repay her in a lump sum, I'm willing to—"

"Shut up." Malone stopped inches from him, but they

were still effectively toe-to-toe. "You want to know what this cost her? I mean *truly* cost her?"

"She gave me the figures, Mr. Malone."

The older man snorted and shook his head, yanking his hat off. Malone tilted his chin back and stared at the ceiling for so long that Ty looked up, too, just to see what he was staring at.

Turned out it was nothing and everything—nothing visible, everything intangible.

"She told you about her brother." Jack Malone's words were half statement, half accusation.

"She did."

"Did she tell you she was the first one to reach him after he and his horse went down?"

A whole new level of understanding hit Ty like a sucker punch to the solar plexus. Clearly, she'd withheld a few critical details from her description of that day.

"I didn't think so," Malone said quietly. "She was thirteen, Mr. Covington. She was thirteen and worshipped her older brother with every cell in her little body." He ran a hand around the back of his neck, the ropy muscles in his forearm tightening as he lowered his chin and glanced at Gizmo again. "I'm going to assume she also left out the part where she tried to perform CPR on Michael and how we had to pry her off him to let the medic get to my son."

"No, sir. She didn't share any of that."

"She wouldn't have."

"May I ask why?"

Malone spared him a short look before shifting so he faced the open barn door. His face had drawn tight, his lips thinning into an almost invisible line. "She witnessed Michael's accident, just like she did yours. She

watched Michael draw his last breath, Mr. Covington."
He faced Ty then. "Just like she did with you."

The world fell out from under Ty. There one moment,
and simply gone the next. He'd known—*known*—that
his heart had failed, that he'd stopped breathing. He
hadn't told anyone for fear they wouldn't believe him.

*But she'd witnessed the whole thing.*

His vision blurred like a snowy TV screen, and Ty
found himself sitting on the ground and being supported
by the very man who'd put him there. Granted, it had
been with words—*truth*—but he was there all the same.

"She thought she'd lost you, Tyson." Malone spoke
so softly that his words were almost swallowed by the
open space in the cavernous barn.

Almost. But not quite.

"She told me she screamed for you. They tried to
get her to leave your side, and the only way they'd let
her stay was if you were tied together somehow. She
knew how much you avoided relationships. She chose the
lesser of what she considered the two evils as you'd see
them—a business partnership. Then you were breathing again, and you pleaded with her to do whatever was
necessary to save your horse. She took you at your word,
spun a few yarns and did exactly as you asked. And what
did you do?" he asked, voice rising. "You emotionally
brutalized her, you jackass! You cast her out!"

Ty choked on the wad of emotions trying to make
their way out of his mouth. There were a hundred, a
thousand things to say. None of them were for this man,
though. He needed to speak to Kenzie. No. Not just
speak to her. He needed to see her. There were things
he had to say. Some of them he didn't understand completely, but he'd figure it out on the way.

Feet on the ground, he leaned forward and propped his forearms on his bent knees. His chin dipped forward. To hell with worrying about pulling on his neck. Her reality was bigger than his fear.

He'd never thanked her. Not really.

Malone must have felt he'd given Ty long enough to process his words because the man pressed on. "She lied, Tyson, but it was for good reason."

"My brothers explained a lot of this. Apparently Eli and Cade decided to offer her breeding rights to Gizmo if she helped me." He looked up then, an unhappy smile pulling at his mouth. "I wasn't the best patient."

"So I heard."

Ty chuffed out a sardonic laugh. "I'm willing to bet she downplayed just how horrible I was." His smile softened. "That's how she is."

"True." Malone sank to the ground beside Ty. The other man's face relaxed a fraction. "You understand she turned them down, your brothers and their offer."

Shame burned his cheeks. "I do."

"Fair enough." The older man looked out over the corrals outside the barn, where several guests were getting ready for a trail ride. He watched them without speaking, seeming to use their activity to distract him as he gathered his thoughts.

Ty was willing to wait. He had enough to think about himself.

He'd accused Kenzie of some horrible things, had taken her money with unintentional disregard to her perpetual worry that it was her money people valued over her.

If he could turn back time, he'd assure her that it was *her* he wanted access to, not her checkbook.

*Access.*

That was really what he'd wanted, what he'd taken for granted. She'd always been there when he wanted her, and it had been more often than not. He'd chafed when she was involved with someone else, blaming it on his temper. But he'd missed that cue, too.

"I'm an idiot," he whispered, shock bleeding through him in a cold rush.

He hadn't been angry.

He'd been *jealous*.

Just as he opened his mouth to explain to The Malone that he needed to call Kenzie, now and not later, the man spoke. Tone quiet and firm, he kept his focus on the ranch guests clambering into borrowed saddles on borrowed horses and having the best time doing it. "Do you understand *why* she couldn't leave your side, why she would have lied, cheated, stolen or worse to ensure she had a place there?"

Ty started to answer, but Malone shook his head. "Think before you answer. Really think, Tyson."

He rubbed his belly in an attempt to soothe his roiling gut. "She felt as if she could make it up to her brother for not being able to save him."

Malone sighed. "You're as big an idiot as I feared." Shifting around to face Ty, he met and held his gaze. "There's no do-over where Michael is concerned. There's no 'making it up to her brother.' Her choices, all of them, were for you."

*Kenzie has his eyes.*

It was all he could think. Well, that and the fact that he missed the hell out of her. She'd been gone twenty-four hours and he wanted her back. Here. With him. If it meant dealing with her overprotective old man in order to get to her, he'd do it. He was going to find a way to pay her back every penny she'd spent plus interest. He wanted, *needed* her to know this had never been about money, that his wanting her here wasn't to secure his financial future. Sure, he was and would always be grateful she'd saved Gizmo's life, but he hadn't asked her to because of the balance in her bank account. He had asked her because he trusted her to do what was necessary, to protect the one thing that meant something to him. *Gizmo.* But that equation was no longer accurate. Over the years, that one thing had become two.

He had his horse.

But now he wanted her.

Shock made him drop his arms. His jaw followed of its own accord.

He'd never wanted a woman in his space. He'd never wanted a woman in his home. He'd never...taken a woman in his own bed. No. Not *a* woman. *The* woman.

It had taken him years, a near tragic event and a painful recovery to realize what this woman meant to him.

He loved Mackenzie Malone.

The Malone was right. He was an idiot.

Seeing recognition set in, Kenzie's dad nodded. "Took you long enough." A small, somewhat sad smile emerged as he stood and offered Ty a hand. They faced each other, nothing but one woman in common. Malone nodded. "See you in Colorado," he said softly. Then he started for his car.

"Thank you, Mr. Malone," Ty called, running out of the barn, already thinking of what he needed to pack, how he'd handle the logistics and how fast he could get on the road.

Malone didn't stop, just raised his hand in acknowledgment. "If I'm going to lose her to you, son, you might as well call me Jack."

KENZIE HAD NO idea where her dad had gone, and her mom was a freaking vault on the subject, offering nothing more than "He had some business to take care of."

So the first day Kenzie was home, she slept. All day. It had been months since she'd had a full night's sleep, and she overindulged. Let the world call her a princess. She didn't care. She'd earned the right to twenty-four hours of solid z's.

She probably could have slept through the second day as well, but she forced herself out of bed. She wanted to see Bean's new foal and get the name recorded so the baby's registration could be filed without delay. She and her father had high hopes for this breeding between one of her program's top mares and a new stud horse from Montana.

Grabbing a small bottle of orange juice as she passed through the kitchen, she also snagged her jacket off the hall tree and then headed outside.

The wind whipped across the plains, biting through her jeans as if they were made of tissue paper and chilling her straight to the bone. Her hand shook as she sipped her juice.

*Should've grabbed coffee.*

A door slammed somewhere ahead, the sound ferried by the wind. She picked up her pace when she saw her dad's pickup parked near the barn's office. With him in residence, the barn should have been a busy place. It was vacant. Someone had left the door at the end of the stable alley open, though. That had turned the alleyway into a wind tunnel, chilling the barn's normally snug interior.

All four of the ranch's border collies were curled up outside the office door, a sure sign her dad was inside. Those dogs followed The Malone everywhere. It was a standing joke around the place that while he was good with horses, he was magic with dogs. Truth was, he was magic with both of them.

She reached for the door, intent on letting herself in, then paused when she realized her father was talking to someone. The wind made it impossible for her to make out the conversation, but one thing was very evident. There were at least two men inside. Someone said something and then there was a third, distinctive voice.

*Three men. One's Dad.*

Had to be horse business. Normally she'd be involved, but after her impromptu return home, he was probably giving her some recovery time. She stepped back over the sleeping dogs and made her way to Bean's stall, stopping several times along the way to scratch a neck or rub an offered nose.

Bean moved to greet her with a soft whuffling noise and a gentle nudge to the shoulder. Deeper in the maternity stall, movement caught Kenzie's eye. A tiny dark foal with a single white sock and a crooked facial blaze lurched to her feet. Unsteady on spindly legs, the little blue roan made her way to her mother's side, nosing the mare as she looked to nurse as a clear reward for her efforts. She suckled for a moment and then turned her attention to the stranger who had captured her mother's attention. Without hesitation and sporting a jaunty step, the foal came forward as confident as could be and sniffed Kenzie's proffered fingertips.

Her heart swelled. "You made a beautiful baby girl, Bean."

The foal nibbled at her fingers, milk teeth blunt but definitely present.

"None of that," Kenzie admonished. Reaching out, she stroked the silky blue-black coat, already dreaming of what the future might hold for such a self-assured little girl. The possibilities seemed endless. It lifted Kenzie's spirits when she'd privately despaired that Ty had broken something in her—something that would take a lifetime or more to repair.

*Ty.*

She missed him. Bad. But the potential between them had been destroyed, erased so efficiently it might have never existed after he kicked her out of his life. The hurt swelled up, pressing against her heart. Her vision blurred with unshed tears. She resented the fact that he could cast her aside as he had, that she was the one who bore all the hurt, all the blame, all of his anger in this. Not for the first time, she wondered what Eli had *told* Ty, if anything, about the brothers' proposition. Had he confessed his own attempt to manipulate the situation? Had he admitted to Ty that she'd shot him down? Or had he taken the easy road and let her be the fall guy? She'd never know, and that bothered her.

How long would she hurt; how long would it be before she stopped loving the man who'd broken her heart?

Bean nudged her again, demanding her attention.

"Sorry, baby." Rubbing the mare's head, she contemplated the foal. She'd need a strong name, something that would resonate on the rodeo circuit. Kenzie grinned. "Baby, you just got named. Lyssa Bean's Domino Effect."

"I like it."

Kenzie physically jumped even as her heart stalled.

Startled, Bean moved between the stranger and her baby, laying her ears back and flicking her tail in agitation.

"Kenzie, please. At least face me."

*That voice. Heaven save me, that* voice.

She shook her head.

Strong but gentle hands rested on her shoulders and encouraged her toward him anyway.

Her shoulders twitched.

His grip tightened.

She drew as deep a breath as her leaden lungs would hold and forced herself to meet the gaze of the man who'd broken her heart.

*Tyson Covington.*

He ran a hand down her arm and wrapped his fingers around hers. "I need to talk to you."

"I, uh…" She cleared her throat, furious at herself for being so soft. "No." She pulled her hand free and side-stepped him, heading for the safety of the office—and her father. "You were pretty clear, Tyson. I got it—*get it*. There's nothing left to say."

He caught up and stepped in front of her. "Yeah, actually there is."

She tried to step around him again but he kept darting in front of her until she finally stopped, glaring at him. "Get out of my way. Or better yet, why don't you try this on for size. It should be familiar enough. Get off my ranch."

He winced.

The urge to comfort him made her want to scream. Shoving past him, she focused on her dad's office door and picked up the pace, certain Ty wouldn't dare move fast enough to catch her. He'd be too worried about reinjury.

That was the only excuse she had for squealing when his hot hand gripped her biceps and pulled her around to face him.

"Stop running." The command was harsh and low.

"Oh, that's rich coming from you," she snapped, pulling free of his grasp. "You, who holds the record for the fastest bed-to-door sprint in the history of lovers worldwide. Go on, Tyson. Show me how it's done."

"In case you missed it, Malone, I ran *to* you, not away."

Her retort stalled, tripping off the end of her tongue in something that sounded suspiciously like "Whumah-ah-ah."

"I have no idea what that means, but I'm going to interpret it as, 'Go ahead, Ty. You have my undivided attention.'" He pulled an envelope from his back pocket and used it to gesture to a short stack of straw bales. "Have a seat. There are a few things I need to say to you."

She sat, not because he ordered her to but because her legs simply gave out.

He dragged a hand down his face. "Thanks."

If she hadn't been so hyperfocused on the surreal moment, she wouldn't have seen the way his hands shook. But she did. Part of her softened toward him at the sight, and she hated herself a little more.

He suddenly broke away from her, then surprised her by walking back and thrusting the envelope at her. "My stamina sucks so I'm on a bit of a timetable here. I had this whole speech worked out, knew exactly what I was going to say, but it never comes out that way, does it? I think it would be easiest to let the paperwork speak for itself."

Kenzie accepted the papers and sat there, staring at the sealed envelope that bore the logo from the legal offices the Malone ranch used for just about everything. "What..." She glanced between the envelope and Ty several times. Swamped with equal parts anxiety and confusion, her mind shut down and her mouth ran off without a map. "You're suing me?"

"What?" Ty shouted, eyes wide. "No! Lord, no. Just... open the damn envelope, Mackenzie. Then I'll explain."

Her hands shook so badly she dropped the envelope. Twice. But she finally got the flap open and pulled out three sheets of paper. The first was a short, handwritten statement.

I, Tyson Hollister Covington, hereby acknowledge the debt owed and the amount established by one Mackenzie Anne Malone in the amount of $112,742.88. I hereby accept responsibility for that debt with the intent to repay it, in full, via a lump-sum settlement. Said settlement shall satisfy all monies and related interest owed.

Ty's signature had been notarized by one Elijah Covington, Esquire.

Her father's hand had added the following:

In recognition of the loan made by the Malone family to one Tyson Covington, the settlement agreement is accepted as proposed.

Below her father's signature, the notary public from the ranch's law firm had affixed his seal.

That had been the third male voice coming from the office.

Fingers numb, she let that sheet drift to the floor. "I didn't lend you the money, Ty. I gave it to you."

"I asked you for it, and we need to be clear before we can move forward. Keep reading."

Kenzie moved on to the next page. It took a second to realize what she was looking at and another to process it. Gasping, she shot to her feet. "No. No, no, no."

He took her by the arms and settled her back on the straw bale. "Yes, Kenzie. Read it."

The registration and ownership for Doc Bar's Dippy Zippy Gizmo had been transferred to her name. She was listed as the horse's sole owner.

She knew her eyes were wild when she met his solemn gaze. "No, Tyson. I can't take Gizmo. I won't. I never wanted this."

"Which is exactly why I'm doing it." He ran a finger along her jaw. "Keep reading."

Hands shaking wildly, her voice vibrated with emotion. "No."

"Please. For me."

"You have no right to ask me to do anything for you. Not anymore."

"I hope to change your mind." He bumped her knee with his. "Now read."

She fought to focus on the third sheet, a letter composed in a surprisingly legible hand—one she recognized from the first page.

Mackenzie,
Sometimes people screw up. Other times they royally screw up. And rarely someone will screw

up so bad that the magnitude of their mistake actually registers on the Richter scale. I've been told that the United States Geological Survey recorded and reported a seismic disturbance day before yesterday. The disturbance was recorded at roughly 10:44 a.m. and was located at 35.9439° N, 104.1931° W. (In case you're curious, that happens to be just outside Roy, New Mexico.) The USGS has said that, based on the available information, their experts believe the event occurred when a total asshole shed every ounce of common sense he allegedly possessed and made a snap judgment. It was the snap judgment and the resulting fallout that caused the disturbance. Apparently, it was the largest event caused by a single individual in recorded history.

You see, I'm the one who set off the Richter scale. I'm the jackass.

I tried to rationalize the event. Apparently the English language hasn't come up with words that convey that particular level of moronic behavior just yet. I'm on it, though, and will let you know when they're available.

Next, I looked for an excuse in a bottle of bourbon. It wasn't there.

I tried to argue with a very wise man who drove over eight hours in crappy weather to come to his daughter's defense. I argued with that man, that father, and told him he'd neglected his daughter by treating her like a poor replacement for the son he'd lost. I have the bruise on my shoulder from the one punch he threw to prove that this man, this father, loves his daughter for all her own strengths

and weaknesses. Nothing more. Nothing less. That
collective experience revealed just how far a good
man will go to ensure his child is protected.

I looked in the mirror then and realized I'm not
a good man. But I want to be.

More important, good or bad, right or wrong, I
want—need to be your man.


Movement made her look up in time to see Ty dig
something out of his pocket and drop to one knee.

"I've talked to your dad. He's a very smart man who
loves you very much. He insisted I call your mom, too,
because apparently she would make my balls into ear-
muffs if I didn't let her get her own threats in before I
set foot on Malone land." He grinned at her. "You might
think you spent the past decade living in your brother's
shadow, but they made it clear to me that they never
felt that way. They love you because you're you, Mac."

The sound that escaped her was far closer to a sob
than she cared to admit, but it was all too much.

Reaching out, he took the letter from her limp fingers
and dropped it at her feet. "I think I remember what the
rest of it says."

"Okay," she whispered, terrified to hope. Despite the
fear, despite the negative voices that told her she was a
fool to lay her heart in this man's hands, she set her hurt
aside, silenced her pride and listened with her heart.

Ty took both her hands in his and stared at her. "This
is harder than I expected it to be."

"The easy road is for cowards and barrel racers."

He grinned. "That's my girl."

Her eyes widened even as her heart tripped and her
breath caught. The way he looked at her, the way his

eyes softened at the sight of her panic, overrode her urge to run.

"That's my girl," he repeated, softer this time. "And that phrase says it all. It sums up all my hopes, my dreams, my desires, wants and needs. It's more than I ever thought to find in this life. If only I'd been smart enough, brave enough, to open my eyes sooner, we could have had all this time together, and I never would have had to listen to you talk about city boy. What was his name? Nashville...Seattle...Buffalo..." He gently pulled her into his embrace.

And she went. Her heart, so broken less than an hour before, had never been so full of love for this man. "Dallas. His name was Dallas."

"Give me a chance to make you forget him, Mac. Give me a chance to wipe out every man who came before and to wipe the floor with any man who believes he has a chance after."

"How long do you think it'll take?" she asked. "My memory's pretty good."

"God willing, darlin', it'll take a lifetime. Just say the word." He lowered his lips to hers, and then waited.

"Yes," she said. "My answer to you will always be yes."

\* \* \* \* \*

# REQUEST YOUR FREE BOOKS!
## 2 FREE NOVELS PLUS 2 FREE GIFTS!

**H** HARLEQUIN®

*Blaze*

### red-hot reads!

**YES!** Please send me 2 FREE Harlequin® Blaze® novels and my 2 FREE gifts (gifts are worth about $10). After receiving them, if I don't wish to receive any more books, I can return the shipping statement marked "cancel." If I don't cancel, I will receive 4 brand-new novels every month and be billed just $4.74 per book in the U.S. or $5.21 per book in Canada. That's a savings of at least 14% off the cover price. It's quite a bargain. Shipping and handling is just 50¢ per book in the U.S. and 75¢ per book in Canada.* I understand that accepting the 2 free books and gifts places me under no obligation to buy anything. I can always return a shipment and cancel at any time. Even if I never buy another book, the two free books and gifts are mine to keep forever.

150/350 HDN GH2D

| | |
|---|---|
| Name | (PLEASE PRINT) |

| | |
|---|---|
| Address | Apt. # |

| | | |
|---|---|---|
| City | State/Prov. | Zip/Postal Code |

Signature (if under 18, a parent or guardian must sign)

### Mail to the **Reader Service:**
**IN U.S.A.:** P.O. Box 1867, Buffalo, NY 14240-1867
**IN CANADA:** P.O. Box 609, Fort Erie, Ontario L2A 5X3

**Want to try two free books from another line?**
**Call 1-800-873-8635 or visit www.ReaderService.com.**

* Terms and prices subject to change without notice. Prices do not include applicable taxes. Sales tax applicable in N.Y. Canadian residents will be charged applicable taxes. Offer not valid in Quebec. This offer is limited to one order per household. Not valid for current subscribers to Harlequin Blaze books. All orders subject to credit approval. Credit or debit balances in a customer's account(s) may be offset by any other outstanding balance owed by or to the customer. Please allow 4 to 6 weeks for delivery. Offer available while quantities last.

**Your Privacy**—The Reader Service is committed to protecting your privacy. Our Privacy Policy is available online at www.ReaderService.com or upon request from the Reader Service.

We make a portion of our mailing list available to reputable third parties that offer products we believe may interest you. If you prefer that we not exchange your name with third parties, or if you wish to clarify or modify your communication preferences, please visit us at www.ReaderService.com/consumerschoice or write to us at Reader Service Preference Service, P.O. Box 9062, Buffalo, NY 14240-9062. Include your complete name and address.

HB15

*Is Matt just a friend? Or a friend…with benefits? Find out!*

Samantha O'Connel grabbed her phone. "What?"

"Huh. That's one way to answer the phone."

It couldn't be—

Matthew Wilkinson. Matt? *Matt!*

Sam hadn't heard his voice in a very long time.

Her eyes shut tight as the world stopped turning. As the memories piled one on top of another. He was her first love. And her first heartbreak.

"Hello? Still there?"

"Hu…hi, Matt?"

"How are you, Sammy?" he asked, his voice dipping lower in a way that made her melt.

No one called her Sammy. It made her blush. "I'm… fine. I'm good. Better."

"Better? Was something wrong?"

"No. I meant to say richer."

He laughed. "I'd kind of figured that after reading about your work."

Her face was so hot she was sure she was going to burst into flames. She was a jumble of emotions. "How are you?" she asked instead.

"I'm good. Jet-lagged. Just in from Tokyo."

"Godzilla stirring up trouble again?"

"I wish," he said, his voice the same. Exactly the same.

She wanted to curl up under the covers and dream about him. "Nothing but boring contracts to negotiate."

"But you still like being a lawyer?"

"Some days are better than others."

"And you're living in New York?"

"I am," he said, the words delivering both disappointment and relief. If he'd moved back to Boston, she would've died. "I heard from Logan last night. He said that crazy apartment of yours is not to be missed."

*Hi there, worst nightmare!* She held a groan. "We haven't talked since you…"

"That's true," he said smoothly. Then he sighed. "I've thought about you. Especially when I've caught yet another article about something you've invented."

She smiled and some of her parts relaxed. Not her heart, though. That was still doing cartwheels. "I'm still me," she said.

"Look, I'm coming to Boston for a few days, and I'd love to stay in that smart apartment. But mostly, I want to see you."

See her? Why? "Um," she said, because she couldn't think straight and this was Matt. "When are you coming?"

"In three days."

*No.* The word she was looking for was *no*. She couldn't see him. Not in a million years. It would be a disaster. "Yeah. I've got some deadline things, but, you know."

He laughed. Quietly. Fondly. And that was what made him so dangerous. He was rich, gorgeous and could have any woman on the planet. The problem was that she'd fallen in love with him two minutes after midnight on her birthday.

"I'm excited to see you, Sammy…"

*Don't miss ONE BLAZING NIGHT by Jo Leigh,*
*available April 2016 wherever*
*Harlequin® Blaze® books and ebooks are sold.*